WITCHING FOR KISMET

PREMONITION POINTE, BOOK 6

DEANNA CHASE

Bayou Moon Press, LLC

www.deannachase.com

Printed in the United States of America

ABOUT THIS BOOK

Carly Preston, a beloved Hollywood star, has lived her life in the spotlight. Most people believe her fifty years on earth has been charmed. She knows better. The tragedy that happened one night over thirty years ago, is never far from her thoughts, though she's learned to let go. But when she receives a message from the past along with a visit from the one person who never wanted to see her again, suddenly it appears that everything that Carly thought about that night is a lie. With the help of Premonition Pointe's coven, Carly is determined to right a wrong, and maybe find a future she never knew she wanted.

CHAPTER ONE

*C*arly Preston stared at Jeremiah Vance as if he'd just grown two heads. "Excuse me? What did you just say?"

The man she hadn't seen or heard from in over thirty years glanced past her shoulder at the people milling around in her oceanside home and frowned. "Is there somewhere more private we can talk?"

Anger rose from the pit of her stomach, and Carly wanted to lash out at the man. She knew he deserved nothing less after he'd just waltzed right up to her door during a wrap party and dropped a bomb on her. But her years of Hollywood media training automatically kicked in, holding her back. If she made a scene in front of more than two dozen Hollywood industry people, the story would be all over the internet within a few hours.

"Fine. Come in. We can go into my office." She held the door open for him, waving him into the house.

He glanced around at the shiny people and scowled but said nothing as she gestured for him to follow her.

Carly's anger started to turn to fury. How dare he judge her and her guests? It wasn't as if he had any experience with Hollywood or the people she associated with when she worked on a movie. As far as she knew, he spent his days holed up in an office crunching numbers for some startup tech company in the Silicon Valley.

Not that she kept tabs on him or anything. Not really, anyway. She just happened to see his name listed in an article about a recent IPO. And from there, she got curious.

As soon as they entered her office and she had the door closed, she turned on him, intending to give him a piece of her mind about his unfair judgment. But when she got a good look at the bone-deep weariness in his eyes, she remembered what he'd said when he'd shocked her stupid. "You said Zane was…" She swallowed hard, unable to get the words out. Carly was certain she'd heard him wrong. It just couldn't be true. Could it? "What was it you said about Zane?"

"I have reason to believe he survived the accident and that he's alive," Jeremiah said, his entire demeanor changing to something she couldn't quite read. Was that determination in his piercing gaze or a thinly veiled accusation?

Carly's hackles rose, but she kept her defensiveness in check. There was no way Jeremiah would show up on her doorstep with such a wild claim unless he was ninety-nine percent certain it was true. She moved to stand next to the window that overlooked the Pacific Ocean, recalling her sister's spirit and her warning that had come out on the patio just moments before Jeremiah showed up on her doorstep.

Changes are coming, Carly. Big changes. And you need to be open to them.

Open. Yeah, okay. Carly could do that. It couldn't hurt to

hear him out, right? She couldn't stop the humorless chuckle that rose from the back of her throat.

Jeremiah narrowed his eyes. "Nothing about this is funny, Carly. Zane has been living a lie for over thirty years."

She cleared her throat. "I know. I wasn't laughing at... You know what? Never mind. It's not important. I'd rather hear about Zane than argue about my inappropriate chuckle." She nodded toward two armchairs that faced her desk. "Can we sit so you can explain what's going on?"

His deep blue eyes flickered to the chairs. After hesitating a moment, he nodded once and strode over to one of the chairs. He sat, leaning forward with his elbows resting on his knees, his hands clasped together.

Carly followed him, and when she took her seat, she turned to face him, waiting expectantly.

"About two weeks ago, a man showed up outside of my office and stopped me when I was leaving work. He was too thin, wearing worn out jeans and a threadbare T-shirt. At first, I thought he was a homeless man looking for money or food and tried to offer him some cash, but he shook his head and said he wasn't looking for a handout. All he wanted was help to free someone named Lazer from an organized crime ring."

"But you're an accountant, not a lawyer, right?" Carly asked.

Jeremiah's eyes widened in surprise. "You know what I do for a living?"

Slightly embarrassed that she'd outed her googling habits, Carly nodded and explained her slightly stalkerish behavior. "I was reading about a new IPO for a startup tech company recently, and when I went to research it, I saw your name mentioned. Something to do with accounting, right?"

He studied her for a moment as if he were trying to figure

something out, and then he shook his head slightly as if to dislodge whatever thoughts he'd been having. "VP of Finance, actually."

"VP. Impressive," Carly said.

He shrugged as if it was no big deal. So much for trying to charm him with compliments.

Ready to move on and eager to find out why Jeremiah thought his brother was alive, she asked, "So what does this guy Lazer have to do with Zane?"

"I didn't know at first. When I told the guy I wasn't a lawyer, he got agitated and said he wasn't looking for one. He was looking for Lazer's brother. But before he could elaborate, he suddenly stiffened as if he were spooked and then ducked into a nearby alley."

"He sounds like someone who was confused," Carly hedged. But there was a prickling feeling in the pit of her stomach that told her the encounter hadn't been a mistake.

Jeremiah cupped the back of his neck with one hand and let out a sigh. "That's what I thought, too. After a small group of businessmen passed me, I checked out the alley and tried to find the man, but he'd disappeared."

Carly furrowed her brow. "Okay. So how did you make the leap to thinking Zane is alive?"

"Two days later, a handwritten note was left in our office mailbox." Jeremiah pulled a carefully folded note out of his pocket and handed it to Carly. "The security footage identified the same thin man who'd tried to talk to me before he got spooked and disappeared. It's already been dusted for prints. There weren't any."

Frowning, Carly took the paper and carefully unfolded it. Just as she opened it up, a tattered photobooth strip of photos slipped out and landed facedown on her hardwood floor. The note read, *He gave this to me and said it would lead me to his loved ones.*

With her heart racing, Carly reached down and picked up the photo strip. She somehow knew what she'd see before she turned it over. Her eyes blurred as she took in the silly photobooth shoot that had been taken just a few hours before the accident that had claimed her twin Caydence and Jeremiah's younger brother Zane. The four of them had piled into the photobooth, with Carly and Caydence sitting on the boys' laps, all of them making faces and laughing with not a worry in the world.

"How…" Carly's voice caught in her throat before she forced out, "This can't be possible. How would that man get this?"

Jeremiah's face pinched as if he were in pain. "There can only be two explanations. Either Zane's wallet was found after his death and someone is trying to play a sick game with us, or he really is alive and needs our help. I don't know about you, but since Zane's body was never found, I have trouble believing his wallet turned up without him. And that means—"

"That you think Zane really is alive," Carly finished for him. Her chest tightened as she tried to imagine what could keep Zane away from her and Jeremiah for over thirty years. Jeremiah was his only family after their mother had passed when Zane was in high school. Their dad had left before Zane was even born. Was it amnesia? But how would he know to tell that other man that these people were his loved ones? Her head started to pound. The chatter and dull roar of party goers in her house had started to rise to an unbearable level. She wanted to stride out into her living room and order everyone to leave.

"I think it's a possibility. And as long as that's true, I'm going to do everything in my power to find this Lazer person. And despite the history between us since the accident, I'm here to ask for your help," he said, holding her gaze.

"My help?" Carly asked, ignoring his reference to their troubled past. She wasn't the one who'd poisoned their relationship. He'd done that all on his own by blaming her for the accident and verbally ordering her out of his house when she'd come to ask him to help her keep the search going. He'd told her she'd done more than enough and that he didn't want to see her again. The coldness in his tone had chilled her to the bone, and just a week after suffering the loss of her sister and her best friend, she'd also lost the boy she'd been half in love with for as long as she could remember. That time in her life had been some of her darkest days, and it wasn't something she cared to think about... ever. Agreeing to help him would mean opening those wounds that she knew hadn't ever really healed, but did she have a choice? Her sister's message was still fresh on her mind. Besides, if there was a possibility that Zane was alive, she'd walk through hell to find him. Only she didn't know exactly what Jeremiah was asking of her. "I'm not sure what I can do, unless you need money for investigators and—"

"I don't need your money, Carly," he snapped and ran a hand through his thick dark hair. "Do you really think I'd come here like this if all I needed was money?"

She shrugged. He wouldn't be the first person to see her as an ATM. But that wasn't what she'd meant. The truth was, she just didn't see how else she could help. "I don't know what would bring you here, Jer. I haven't heard from you in over thirty years. How do I know what your motivations are?"

His eyes narrowed, and she could see he was getting his hackles up again.

Carly raised a hand, stopping him from voicing whatever

was on the tip of his tongue. "I just don't know how else I can help. I'm not a private investigator. How exactly am I supposed to help you find this Lazer person with so little to go on?"

"The Premonition Pointe coven. The authorities are refusing to help me. They say Zane's case is closed. And without more evidence, a PI isn't going to get very far. I think we need witches who can use... more *unconventional* methods to solve a case like this," he said. "You're friends with Joy Lansing, right? The one you did that movie with? I want you to ask them to help me find Zane."

Carly opened her mouth to answer, to tell him that while they were friends, that was one hell of a big ask, especially since Joy had already helped her find her niece, Harlow, after she'd been abducted. But before she could get the words out, a scream came from outside, followed by the squeal of tires as a car sped off into the night.

"Someone call 911!" she heard one of her guests call out.

Without hesitation, Carly burst out of the office and ran toward the front door where a number of her guests were gathered. "What happened?"

"Hit and run. A black SUV just ran someone down who was crossing the street," Vanessa, one of her young co-stars explained.

"Who is it? Who's been hit?" she asked, already pushing her way through the small crowd to get out the front door.

"No idea," Vanessa said from behind her.

Carly slipped away from the gawkers in front of her house and ran toward the person sprawled in the middle of her street. He was a thin man with sandy-blond hair, ripped jeans and a blood-stained T-shirt. She frantically searched for the wound, and when she found a hole in his right shoulder, she swore and used the sweater she'd been wearing to try to stop the bleeding. Not only had he been run down, but someone had shot him.

A gasp came from behind her. Carly twisted her head to see Jeremiah staring down at the man in horror. "It's him. The guy who tried to talk to me in front of my office."

CHAPTER TWO

*E*xhaustion swept over Carly as she shifted in the plastic seat in the waiting room of the hospital. It had been hours since the hit and run had occurred in front of her house. She'd stayed with the man until the paramedics arrived, keeping her hand over his wound the entire time. Once they'd gently pushed her aside, Jeremiah had wrapped an arm around her shoulder and pulled her into his side, comforting her.

She'd been in so much shock that she hadn't even questioned the move. Now that hours had passed, she wondered if he'd even realized what he was doing. The last time he'd touched her had been the day they'd both lost their siblings.

"I brought you this," Jeremiah said, sitting in the seat beside her and handing her a paper cup.

The scent of fresh coffee filled her senses, making her almost weep with relief. "Thank you," she said and closed her eyes as she took a long sip. Even stale hospital coffee was heaven to her tastebuds. Closing her eyes, she let out a contented sigh, happy to have at least one creature comfort while they waited.

"Any word?" he asked.

Carly shook her head. "He's still in surgery. The nurse said he didn't have an ID on him either. They're hoping when he wakes up that he can tell them who he is."

Jeremiah slumped back into his chair, his shoulders hunched and his eyes weary. "So we're not likely to know anything for several more hours."

"Not likely," Carly said. "We should probably go get some sleep, but I just can't leave until I know he's okay."

"I can't leave until I get some answers," Jeremiah said.

Carly gave him the side-eye. Someone had clearly just tried to murder him, to silence him. Why else would they shoot him and run him down inside Carly's exclusive neighborhood? Things like that didn't usually happen in the cliffside community she'd called home for the past six months. "I know you're anxious about what he knows about Zane, but I doubt he's going to be in any position to talk to us anytime soon."

"I know that. But what if his attackers come back?" Jeremiah stared at the double doors that led to the ICU, where they'd take the man after his surgery. "Someone needs to stand guard, make sure he's safe. And I'm fairly positive the local police force isn't going to do that."

Carly nodded and pulled out her phone. Five minutes later, she ended the call and turned to Jeremiah. "My security team is on it. They are sending someone over ASAP, and he'll have twenty-four-hour protection until I say otherwise."

Jeremiah blinked at her. "Just like that? You have a security team who will come as soon as you make one phone call?"

She shrugged. "You might not be aware of this, Jer, but

because of my job, I'm fairly well-known. Do you know what that means for women in the entertainment industry?"

"That you have a lot of annoying fans?" he asked, looking irritated.

She huffed out a breath and rolled her eyes. "Yes, fans. But more importantly, the more famous an actress is, the more unstable people she attracts. When I'm in LA, I always have a security team around. When I'm in Premonition Pointe, I just have Jake over there." She nodded to the man sitting a few rows away who was fiddling with his phone.

"Jake?" Jeremiah asked, looking astonished. "He's with you?"

Jake looked up at the sound of his name and gave Jeremiah a slight smile. Then he went back to studying his phone.

"I wouldn't say *with* me. More like just keeping an eye on me. When I first came to Premonition Pointe, there seemed little reason for security. The people in this town don't really care much about my job or the Oscars on my mantle. Or if they do, they are polite enough to let me just live my life without all the fuss of stardom. But after Harlow's abduction, neither of us have felt save without someone around to make sure nothing like that happens again. So Jake follows me, Mikey follows Harlow, and we both pretend like it's normal instead of an over-the-top reaction to the crazy people of the world."

"I don't think it's over-the-top," Jeremiah said softly as he wrapped an arm around her shoulders and pulled her in for a sideways hug. "I heard about what happened with your niece. That must've been terrifying."

"It was. And like you said, local law enforcement was less than helpful. If it wasn't for Joy and the coven, I have no idea if we'd have ever found her." She leaned into him, soaking up his warmth and comfort and familiarity. Even after all the years that had passed, she still felt like home was in the arms of a Vance boy. She let out a small contented sigh and laid her head on his shoulder.

After a few moments, Jeremiah stared down at her and asked, "The coven helped you before. Do you think they'll help us now?"

Carly didn't say anything at first. It was a lot to ask the Premonition Pointe coven to help them try to determine who this man was and why he'd left Jeremiah an old picture from the day Zane was lost in the boating accident. As far as she knew, he was just another crazy person trying to get attention from a Hollywood star. Was it possible this guy used Jeremiah to get to her? She hated that she thought that way, but after thirty years in the business, she'd be naïve not to at least consider it.

"Carly, if there's any chance that Zane's actually alive, we have to pursue this," he said quietly, his voice gruff with emotion.

Tears stung her eyes again because she knew he was right. No matter how much it might rip their hearts out when they found out all of this was a wild goose chase, there was no way she could walk away without knowing the truth. She sat up straight, disentangling herself from his embrace. "You're right. But all the women of the coven lead busy lives. I'm sure at least Joy would help out, if not all of them, but can't we wait until we can at least talk to this man before we start scouring the state for Zane? How do we even know where to start?"

Jeremiah let out an audible breath as the fight seemed to leave him. "I guess you're right. I just… It's been a very long time, Carly. It's hard for me to think that he's been alive but lost all this time. If there's a chance… I just want to get him back as soon as possible."

Her heart ached at his words. She'd feel the same way about her sister. Hell, she felt the same way about Zane. He had been her best friend after all. "I know. We just—"

"Ms. Preston?" a woman in scrubs called from near the nurse's station.

"Yes?" Carly hopped up and hurried over to the woman with Jeremiah on her heels.

"Hello, I'm Dr. Green, the surgeon for John Doe. I understand you were with him when he came in?" the woman asked.

"Yes," Carly said. "He was shot and run down in front of my house. I stayed with him until the paramedics arrived."

She frowned. "So you're not related to him in any way?"

Carly shook her head. "No, but we're very concerned about him and wanted to wait to be sure he's going to be okay."

Dr. Green pursed her lips together. "Since you're not a relative, I can't release any information about the patient. Do you have any idea how we might get in touch with his family?"

"We don't even know his name," Jeremiah said, a note of irritation in his voice. "No one does."

"That's unfortunate." Dr. Green made a note in the chart she was holding. "I'm sorry I can't be more helpful, but—"

Carly pasted on an understanding smile and placed a light hand on the surgeon's arm. Her industry training kicked in, and she prayed she was able to sway this woman with a little bit of Hollywood shine. "I completely understand the position you're in. But do you think you could just tell us if he made it? Jeremiah and I are very concerned, and I'm not sure either of us will be able to sleep until we know he at least has a fighting chance."

Dr. Green's gaze flickered from Carly to Jeremiah and back again. Finally, she let out a small sigh. "I guess it won't hurt to let you know that he made it out of surgery, but he's not out of the woods yet. If he wakes up in the next twenty-four to forty-eight hours, then we'll have a better understanding of what we can expect for his recovery."

"If he wakes up?" Carly asked, her hand tightening slightly on the woman's arm.

Dr. Green laid her other hand over the top of Carly's and whispered, "He sustained a head injury as a result of the hit and run. That's what we're most concerned about." Then she stepped back and straightened her shoulders. "Thank you for what you did for John Doe tonight. Without your quick assistance, he likely wouldn't have lived long enough to see the inside of the ER."

Carly nodded and thanked the doctor in return. After the surgeon disappeared back through the ICU doors, Jeremiah stared at her. "What?" she asked.

"Do you do that all the time?" he asked.

She raised her eyebrows in question.

"Oh, come on, Carly," he said, shaking his head. "You just charmed that information right out of her. I guess it really helps to be an actress when you want something."

His tone had been more matter-of-fact than accusatory, but the statement still stung. He made it sound as if she manipulated people for sport. "We needed to know if he was alive, right?"

"Yes," he said with a nod.

"Well, I got you that information. There's no need to make me feel guilty about my methods." She turned and started walking toward the exit.

"Carly, wait!" he called after her.

"I'm going home to get some rest." She gestured to the man standing next to her bodyguard, Jake. "Phil over there will make sure no one gets access to John Doe without us knowing about it."

Without waiting for a reply, she fled the hospital, determined to put some distance between her and Jeremiah Vance. How was it that he could make her feel safe one minute, as if he really cared about her, and then judged for her profession the next? She'd had enough men in her life treat her as if her career made her vapid and undeserving of respect. She would not accept that same treatment from him. It didn't matter that he was Zane's brother and the one other person who would move heaven and earth to find him.

CHAPTER THREE

Carly was still irritated when she walked into her home a half hour later. Sure, she was upset with Jeremiah's reaction to how she went about getting answers about John Doe, but more importantly, she was upset with herself for letting him get to her. She was a highly successful woman in her early fifties. The days of longing for anyone else's approval were long gone. Or at least they should be. Why was she letting Jeremiah get under her skin?

"Carly? Is that you?" The distinct voice of Joy Lansing called from somewhere inside her home.

"Joy? Are you still here?" Carly hurried through the kitchen. She'd parked in the garage and entered through a side door, unaware that anyone might still be in her home from the night before. It was mid-morning. Surely everyone else had left, right? Her nerves started to kick in to overdrive. When she rounded the corner, she spotted Joy sitting on the couch with Harlow. They each had a mug in hand, and there was a box of scones on the coffee table. Carly let out a sigh of relief as her shoulders relaxed. She just didn't have the energy to deal with anyone else.

"Hey," Joy said as she stood, gesturing for Carly to take her place. "Take a seat. I'll get you a mug of hot chocolate."

"Bless you," Carly said as she gratefully sank into the couch.

Joy handed her a scone before she disappeared into the kitchen.

As Carly moved to take a bite, she glanced at her niece and noticed for the first time her red-rimmed eyes and haunted expression. She dropped the scone and moved closer to Harlow. "Hey, what is it? What happened?"

Tears filled the younger woman's eyes and spilled unchecked down her cheeks. She pressed a hand over her eyes and muttered, "Sorry."

Carly scooted closer and wrapped her arms around Harlow, smoothing her blond curls. "There's nothing to be sorry about."

"I didn't... want... to lay this on you," she forced out through her tears.

"You don't need to hide anything from me. You know that." Carly pulled away and gently wiped her tears. "What's wrong? How can I help?"

She shook her head. "I just... had a bad night. After that man was attacked, it brought everything back."

Carly knew she meant the night she was abducted, when she'd been stolen from the very same home they lived in now. Tightening her hold on Harlow, she whispered, "Oh, honey. I'm so sorry."

Harlow held on tightly, as if she never wanted to let go.

They sat there together, just hanging onto each other as Carly reassured her that she was safe. That she'd make sure nothing like that would ever happen again, wanting to reassure her yet again, that she wasn't alone. As a child, Harlow had witnessed her father, Carly's half-brother, choking her mother and had shot him. Harlow's mother had lied to the police about what had happened, and forced Harlow to never speak of it again. The entire ordeal had caused years of unresolved trauma, leaving Harlow with no father and an estranged mother. She was in therapy to deal with everything that happened to her, and most days she handled everything well. But obviously the attack had been a trigger.

When Harlow's tears finally dried, Carly pulled back and gently asked her, "Do you want me to get you an emergency appointment with your therapist?"

Harlow shook her head. "No. I'm seeing her at the end of the week. I think I just needed to let myself process a bit."

"Anyone would," Carly assured her.

"I think I'm going to go get a shower and then take a nap." Harlow stood and then leaned down to kiss her aunt on the cheek. "Thank you. I don't think you truly understand just how much being with you helps when I'm going through one of these meltdowns."

Carly reached out and squeezed her niece's hand. "Everyone needs someone they can count on. I'm that person for you."

Harlow nodded. Then she narrowed her eyes as she studied her aunt. "Carly?"

"Yeah?"

"Who's that person for you?" Harlow asked, her gaze full of concern.

Carly almost chuckled, but it would've been a humorless one. She knew Harlow was aware that she didn't have very many true friends. Ones that she could say anything to, that she considered a ride-or-die type person. Caydence and Zane had been those people for her. But after she'd lost both of them, she'd all but shut down in the friend department. Sure, she had people she called friends, acquaintances she spent time with at the spa or joined them out at lunch, that sort of thing. But there was no one she could call on and trust with her most vulnerable secrets. But maybe that was changing since she now had Joy and the rest of the coven in her life. She gave her niece a soft smile. "It's you, Harlow. Don't you know that?"

"Carly..." Harlow's eyes welled again, but this time she smiled through her tears. "I love you."

"I love you, too, sweet girl." The emotion overwhelming Carly made her chest tighten, and she placed her hand over her heart, trying to get herself to relax.

Harlow kissed her aunt on her cheek again and then excused herself to go shower and take a nap.

Carly watched her go, wishing with everything she had that she could ease Harlow's pain. She'd gladly take it on if it meant Harlow could be free of the trauma that had plagued her for so long.

Joy appeared, holding a tray with a fluffy omelet and a couple of mugs. "I thought you might need something other than a scone."

"Bless you," Carly said, as her mouth watered at the breakfast she hadn't even realized she wanted. "You're a goddess."

"So are you." Joy sat across from her in one of the armchairs and grabbed one of the mugs of hot chocolate. "I would've brought this out sooner, but I didn't want to interrupt your time with Harlow. She had a rough night. As soon as you left, she started to unravel."

Carly took a sip of the rich hot chocolate, grateful for the shot of sugar in her veins. But then Joy's words sank in. "Have you been here the entire time?"

Joy nodded. "She needed someone, and I had no idea when you'd get back." She shrugged. "It wasn't a problem. Troy dropped off the scones on his way to a photoshoot."

"You're an angel. You know that, right?" Carly reached over and squeezed her hand. "Thank you. And thank Troy for me. That was sweet of him. I know you two don't get a ton of time together."

"I can see the boyfriend later today or tomorrow. You know I'd do anything for you and Harlow." Joy gave her a soft smile, and Carly was certain the other woman would never know just how much the moment meant to her.

After dabbing at her eyes and clearing her throat, Carly said, "Make sure you let me know how I can repay you."

This time Joy pursed her lips and shook her head. "You don't need to repay me anything, Carly."

"But—"

Joy held her hand up, her expression troubled. "We're friends, right?"

"Of course. I just—"

"No. That's enough. I stayed without an ounce of hesitation because I care about both you and Harlow. Understand? I don't want to hear any more talk about repayment."

Carly almost chuckled at the willowy blonde. She was using her mom voice, the one intended to shut down a conversation. "Understood," Carly said with a nod. "It's hard to remember sometimes that Premonition Pointe isn't like Hollywood. That town runs on favors. No one does anything without knowing what they'll get out of it. Or at least that's the way it seems. That's part of the reason that I moved here. To get away from the industry and the kind of people who are always working an angle."

"I get it," Joy said, her eyes crinkling at the edges. "You forget that I've worked with some of them, too. But you don't have to worry about any of that here, because with myself and the other coven members, you've got a family here who'd drop everything if you needed them to."

It was now or never. Carly could feel it in her bones. Jeremiah's voice kept echoing in her head that they'd need the coven's help. But it was Zane's face she saw when she asked, "Do you think the coven would be willing to help me find someone who's been... out of touch for over thirty years?"

"You mean like track them down for you?" Joy asked, frowning. "Isn't that what private detectives are for?"

"Normally yes, but we have very little to go on," Carly said. "Like almost nothing. I was hoping maybe we could try that finding spell you all did before when you tracked down Harlow, or the one we did recently to locate Kade for Iris."

Joy bit her lip. "Do you have anything connected to this person?"

"His brother and a photo Zane's supposedly been carrying around this entire time." Carly held her breath, knowing she was asking a lot. The spell was a longshot at best. She knew that. Plus, it took a lot of energy to execute the type of spell she was asking for, and they didn't exactly have confirmation that Zane was still alive. Sure, Caydence had warned her that she needed to be open to changes, and she was definitely trying, but that didn't mean that Zane really was alive. This could be a wild goose chase that ended in an entirely different way than they hoped.

"Okay then. I'm game," Joy said with a kind smile. "I'll have to ask the others, but I'm sure they'd be willing to help. Do you have the photo here?"

Carly shook her head. She'd given it back to Jeremiah along with the note.

"Too bad," Joy said. "I've been working on accessing my visions. It's still very hit or miss, but I'd be up for trying."

"That would be..." Carly yawned right in the middle of her sentence as exhaustion kicked in again. "Oh, sorry. That would be great."

Joy patted her knee and stood. "We all need some rest. How about I give you a call tomorrow and we'll figure out a good time to try some things?"

"You're an angel," Carly said and rose to hug her friend. "You know if there's ever anything I can do for you, all you have to do is say the word."

"You've already done more than enough," Joy said, her tone quiet and full of sincerity. "The support you gave me while we were filming our movie is something I'll never forget. I was so green and totally out of my element, but you were there with advice and a kind word all the way through it. I swear I'd have blown that role if it hadn't been for you."

Carly felt her eyes misting over again and had to take a moment to calm herself before she wrapped her arms around Joy in another hug. "You're more than welcome for anything that I did to help, but make no mistake, you're a wonderful actress. While it might have taken you a little longer to learn your marks, the acting has been there from the start. I refuse to take the credit for any of that success. Understand?"

Joy nodded and squeezed Carly tighter. "I can't believe you're so humble. No one else in Hollywood even comes close."

Carly laughed as she released her. "Most of them are just

trying to stay relevant. My secret is that I just don't care that much anymore. I'll take on roles I think are interesting, but the truth is that I don't really need to work these days. I could just stay in my herb studio all day, every day for the rest of my life, never sell a single thing, and I'd be just fine. It's a privileged place to be. But it also makes it so that I don't have to worry about my next role, which, to be honest, is even more freeing than I ever imagined."

"I'm so happy for you, Carly," Joy said, sounding as if she meant it. So many others in her profession wouldn't have.

"Honestly, me too," Carly said with a chuckle as she walked Joy to the door. "Get some rest and we'll talk tomorrow."

"Same to you, but don't hesitate to call if something urgent comes up, okay?"

Carly promised to call if there was any development with their John Doe. Then she shut the door behind her friend and leaned against it with her hand over her heart. It had been a long time since she'd met someone she'd call a true friend, but she was certain that Joy Lansing had stepped right into that role way back when she'd been helping Carly find Harlow. But Carly hadn't realized just how strong that bond really was until that moment. Her heart swelled in her chest, making her ache with the intensity of it all.

Pushing the fear aside that she'd somehow lose this friend too, she allowed herself a small smile as she retreated to her bedroom and climbed into bed. When she woke up eight hours later, she didn't even remember her head hitting the pillow.

CHAPTER FOUR

After grabbing a light dinner, Carly found herself in her herb studio, staring at her stash of ingredients lining the wall. She always seemed to find herself in there when she was restless. Creating new potions was the one thing that managed to occupy her mind when she was anxious about something. The details around John Doe and Zane seemed too fantastical to be real, and yet, the man that had tried to speak with Jeremiah about his brother was now in the hospital after an attempt on his life.

Her gut said there was a lot more to the story, and in her heart, she knew she'd have to find a way to uncover the truth of the mystery, or else she'd always wonder if it was true that Zane was alive. And if there was even one ounce of hope that he hadn't died that day, she'd go to the ends of the earth to find him.

Because her mind had been occupied with thoughts of Zane and her sister over the past twenty-four hours, it had reminded Carly that she'd started to forget details of the two people she'd loved most in the world up until that point. She especially couldn't remember most of the details of the day when she'd lost both of them. How was it possible that Zane might still be alive? If only she could remember exactly what happened that day.

Scanning her shelves, Carly reached for her stores of lemon bark, rosemary, and ginkgo. Using her pestle and mortar, she ground the herbs separately and then left her studio. She returned five minutes later with pictures of both Zane and Caydence as well as a compass that Zane had given her on graduation day and a charm bracelet that had belonged to her sister. If she was going to do a memory spell, she'd need something to connect herself to each of them. But first she had to see if she even had the ability to form the spell.

Carly had always known she had some magical ability, but it had taken years for her skills to develop enough that she was actually able to make a potion or cast a spell. It seemed that her magic developed with age. That wasn't a bad thing. She shuddered to think of what she would've done when she was younger if she'd had the ability to make a powerful spell. Now that she was older, she was more deliberate and careful with what she experimented with.

After retrieving her mini cauldron, Carly filled the container with water that was sourced from a special spring from Keating Hollow, a magical town that was north of Premonition Pointe. Carly had been there once and had been charmed by the quaint downtown and the friendly witches who lived there.

After bringing the water to a boil, she added her ingredients and turned the burner on low, giving the herbs time to steep. When the potion turned a mossy green color, she wrinkled her nose and turned off the burner. It was time to work her magic.

She sat on a stool with the potion in front of her and stared into the dull liquid. The faint tug of power materialized in her gut, and she focused on it, willing the feeling to grow. The magic spread from her stomach to her chest and then tickled her skin as it shot down to her fingertips.

Carly smiled to herself. That was getting easier. She grabbed her wooden spoon, dipped it into the potion, and chanted, "From the dark, behold the light. Unlock the past, find the missing link, and let the memories flow at once with just a drink."

Gentle sparks of magic curled around the wooden spoon and inched toward the liquid. The moment the magic connected with the liquid, the potion turned bright yellow and glowed with her magic. She stirred faster, making sure the potion set, and when she pulled the wooden spoon out of the liquid, the glow vanished, transforming the potion into something that resembled lemonade.

Carly lifted the potion and sniffed. She grinned when the faint scent of vanilla filled her senses. Memory spells should always smell like one of the practitioner's earliest memories, regardless of the ingredients used. Vanilla always reminded Carly of her grandmother, who had taken her and Caydence in after their mother died in a tragic accident before their first birthday. Their dad had already moved on to his second wife and claimed he couldn't afford to take them. He'd been mostly absent from their lives and had only shown an interest in Carly once she'd become famous. That's when she'd met her half-brother. The only thing good he'd ever been responsible for was Harlow. She was thankful for her but hadn't had any use for her brother, who turned out to be even worse than her father.

Carly sniffed the potion again and smiled. Her Grandma

Cece had used vanilla as her perfume right up until she passed away in her early seventies. The scent always comforted her.

"Success!" Carly cried, holding up her latest achievement. She was just about to test out her potion when she heard her doorbell. She glanced at the clock. It was close to nine o'clock at night. She wasn't expecting anyone. But maybe Harlow had invited someone over.

A knock sounded on her studio door a few seconds later. "Aunt Carly?"

"Come on in," Carly called to Harlow as she cleaned up her workstation.

Her niece poked her head in. "Jeremiah Vance is here to see you."

"He is?" Carly asked as she strode toward the door, suddenly anxious to find out what he wanted. Was John Doe awake?

"I left him at the door," Harlow said with an amused smile. "But if I'd realized how much you wanted to see him, I'd have invited him in and offered him a drink."

It was good to see her niece feeling better even if it was at her expense. "There's nothing going on. Not like *that* anyway." Carly rolled her eyes. "Don't jump to conclusions."

"Sure, Auntie." Harlow winked and then disappeared upstairs as Carly headed for the door. She opened it to find Jeremiah standing there with his back to her as he stared at her quiet street.

"Jeremiah?" Carly asked.

"You've built a wonderful life for yourself," he said without turning around to look at her.

"Uh, okay," she said, frowning. He sounded... different. Subdued and reflective.

He finally turned to look at her. "Your niece is really lovely."

That got a smile out of her. "She really is. Did you want to come in?"

Jeremiah nodded once and followed her into the house.

Carly led the way to her kitchen and waved at the small breakfast table that looked out over the ocean. "Have a seat and I'll get you something to drink."

He did as she said and stared out the window at the moonlit sea.

"Coffee?" she asked. "I have some Irish Cream to go with it."

"Sounds perfect," he said.

She nodded and got to work brewing a fresh pot of coffee. As she waited for the coffee maker to finish, she pulled out some desserts that had been left over from the party the night before. Once she had everything on the table, she sat across from him and handed him a mug.

"You're really quite the hostess," he said, eyeing the tray of various desserts. "What is that? Chocolate torte?"

She nodded. "Chocolate torte, caramel bars, and key lime pie cheesecake."

Jeremiah groaned as he reached for the chocolate dessert.

Carly sipped her doctored coffee and smiled to herself as she watched him enjoy the rich dessert.

"You're not having any?" he asked when he was almost finished with his piece.

"Maybe later. The Irish coffee is good for now."

"I bet you don't eat much dessert, being an actress an all."

She shrugged. He wasn't wrong. At her age, it was tough maintaining a figure that didn't offend directors who were already predisposed to hire younger actresses. And although she'd stopped worrying so much about pleasing anyone in her profession lately, it was hard to let go of old insecurities. It was likely she'd never stop watching what she ate out of sheer habit, just like she'd always automatically get on her treadmill first thing in the morning. If she didn't, she felt out of sorts all day.

"If you ask me, I think it's time you started enjoying yourself more," Jeremiah said.

She chuckled. "What makes you think I don't enjoy myself?"

He shrugged. "Just a hunch."

While she'd been quick to dismiss him, the truth was that until she moved to Premonition Pointe, she hadn't much enjoyed herself. There were moments when she was working on a movie that she loved, or spending time with Harlow or even with a few friends, but things had changed when she'd moved to her home in the small beach town. She'd started to really enjoy her space, her herb studio, the grounded feeling she got from the beach below, and of course the coven members. For the first time in a long time, she was starting to feel like she was where she belonged. Carly looked him in the eye and said, "Maybe you can help me with that."

His lips quirked. "Maybe I will."

They sat in a companionable silence for a few minutes while Jeremiah finished his torte and Carly sipped her coffee. Finally, when he was done and pushed the plate away, Carly asked, "Jeremiah?"

"Yeah?"

"Why did you come here tonight?"

"I…" He glanced at the moonlit night once more before turning back to her. "I just needed to be close to someone who loved Zane."

CHAPTER FIVE

*C*arly reached across the table and placed her hand over Jeremiah's. "I understand."

Jeremiah's gaze flicked to their hands. "Are you sure? I'm probably intruding." He glanced at the clock on the wall and let out a humorless laugh. "It's nine-thirty. I realize you Hollywood types have a reputation for parties and late nights, but somehow I doubt that's really your scene."

It was Carly's turn for a humorless laugh. "The only time I have parties is when I have one for the cast of one of my movies after we're all done. Wrap parties are a tradition, and if I throw it, it means I can control the environment. My parties rarely end up in the tabloids because there's really nothing to report. However, I bet they are having a field day with John Doe."

"You don't know for sure?" he asked with a raised eyebrow.

"Nope. I haven't looked. I'm sure if there's something I need to know my publicist will make sure I'm informed."

"That's probably for the best." He drained the last of his Irish coffee and placed the mug back on the table. "You were probably in the middle of something. I should get out of your hair and let you have your evening back."

"You didn't interrupt anything," Carly said quickly, not quite sure why she didn't want him to leave. Maybe it was because for the first time in over thirty years, they actually seemed comfortable in each other's presence. She wasn't ready for it to end. "I'd actually just finished working on a memory potion."

"Memory potion?" he parroted in surprise. "Are you saying you have the power to make something like that?"

"Yep. I'm sort of a late bloomer," she said, her pride making her beam at him. "While Caydence always was able to do magic, my power was dormant until a few years ago. Or at least that's when I discovered I was gifted at herbs and started to suspect it wasn't my green thumb that was making them thrive."

"Wow," he said, seemingly impressed. "Isn't that sort of unusual?"

"Maybe? It's not unheard of if that's what you mean. Anyway, want to see my herb studio?"

"Sure."

Carly led the way through her house to her sanctuary, and when she waved him inside, she stood back, watching as his expression turned from surprise to delight when he turned and spotted all the pots of thriving herbs.

"You grew all of these?" he asked, reaching over and inspecting the bloom on her rose hip plant.

"Every last one." Carly leaned against the doorjamb and watched as he took in her nursery and then the jars of dried herbs lining her walls.

"Nobody knows that you do this, do they?" he asked, turning to meet her gaze.

"The coven members know." It wasn't something that she advertised. Too much of her life was already played out in the media. She didn't need reporters speculating about her powers. "This is just for me. I'd rather not share it with the public."

"Understandable." He let out a soft chuckle and shook his head. "I'm an idiot."

Well, that was interesting. "Why?"

He sat on the stool at her workbench. "All of these years, I thought… Well, it doesn't matter what I thought. Let's just say you're not the person I made you out to be in my mind."

Carly tensed. She could only imagine what he'd thought of her life. He'd already blamed her for Zane's death. If he'd followed her life that was reported by the tabloids, he likely thought she'd had multiple high-profile affairs and had been a demanding, difficult actress who was passed over for movies because of her attitude. There wasn't any truth to the former. She'd had one high-profile relationship with a costar, but it only lasted until he fell in love with his next costar. After that, she'd been careful about who she dated, and had stayed away from actors.

The accusation of being difficult, well, she owned that one. Because Carly Preston wasn't going to be pushed around, harassed, or used by anyone. After she'd put a celebrated director in his place when he'd expected her to share his bed, she'd spent years taking smaller roles and signing on to indie movies in order to find work. But because of that, she earned the reputation of a consummate professional and two Oscars. After that, she'd been the one to say who would be working on a movie if a producer wanted her. Not the other way around. Carly had been lucky in her career, but she'd also worked extremely hard to get where she was and had earned her right to that kind of influence.

"Carly?" Jeremiah said. "I'm sorry. I shouldn't have said anything."

She waved a hand, indicating they didn't need to talk about it. "Forget it. The press can be very misleading. I'm used to it." He winced, but Carly pressed on. "Anyway, let's talk about that memory potion. Care to test it out with me?"

"You want me to try your memory potion?" he asked, looking skeptical.

"You're not scared, are you?" she teased as she picked up the potion and poured some into two cups.

"Scared? No, but…"

"But what?" she asked, fully expecting him to back out. Honestly, she couldn't blame him. If someone she barely knew tried to get her to try their homemade potion, she'd decline without a second thought.

"You're trying to bait me, aren't you?" he asked with a wry smile.

"A little bit." She retrieved the pictures, the compass, and the charm bracelet she'd left on her desk and placed them on her workbench. "You don't have to join me, but since you've arrived and brought everything back up, I realized that I'm having trouble remembering details of the day we lost Caydence and Zane. So I wanted to try this memory potion to help me recall all the details, see if there's something I've missed. Maybe find a reason to believe that Zane survived."

Jeremiah didn't say anything for a long moment. Finally, he nodded. "That's a good idea. Let's do it."

Surprise rushed through her, and she slowly sat on a stool as she processed the fact that Jeremiah Vance, the man who'd blamed her for his brother's death for so many years, trusted her enough to try her potion. "Are you sure?"

"Positive." He nodded at the items in front of her. "Are we supposed to do something with those?"

Feeling like a small part of her had healed, she stood and handed him the compass. "Zane gave this to me. Hold onto it and use it to connect with him."

Jeremiah held it in his palm and closed his fingers around it. "Did you know our grandfather gave this to him?"

"What? You can't be serious." Carly gasped out. "I thought he got it from that antique shop he liked so much."

"Very serious. Gramps told him the compass would always help him find his way home." Jeremiah grimaced and let out a curse. "If Zane gave it to you, I think that means he thought you were his home."

"I'm sorry," Carly said, feeling like she'd just taken something from him. "I had no idea."

"Of course you didn't," Jeremiah said softly. "How could you?" He straightened as he added, "There's nothing to be sorry about. If this is anyone's fault, it's mine." Carly started to ask for clarification, but he cut her off. "Let's do this. I'd really like to visit my brother again."

"Okay. Let's do it." Carly fingered Caydence's charm bracelet and with her other hand, she added a drop of the potion to each of their pictures. "All you have to do is focus on Zane as you drink the potion. Then wait for a vision to appear."

"Got it." He glanced once more at the compass and then swallowed the potion.

Carly rubbed the sunflower on the charm bracelet and followed suit. Her skin started to tingle immediately as magic crawled up her arms, shimmering as if she were kissed by moonlight.

"Whoa," Jeremiah breathed.

She glanced at him, finding his eyes wide and his face full of wonder.

"You look… gorgeous."

Over her career, Carly had been told she was gorgeous hundreds of times. But the awe in Jeremiah's eyes and in his tone filled her up and made her feel as if someone was really seeing her for the first time ever. She started to thank him, but then her world shifted and suddenly Zane appeared beside Jeremiah.

Her best friend grinned at her and mouthed, *Ask him!*

You're crazy, she mouthed back, just like she had that day they'd been boating. His eyes sparkled, and he whispered something to Jeremiah that made him turn to look at her curiously.

"Caydence?" Carly called and turned right into her sister who had appeared beside her.

"You bellowed?" her sister teased.

Carly frowned at the ghostly image. While Zane appeared to be a fully realized person, Caydence was just an outline of herself and sort of shimmering in the light. She wanted to ask her why, but instead she repeated her words from years ago. "Let's go swimming."

And right there it was. That statement was the reason Jeremiah believed the accident was all her fault. Still, the memory continued on, forcing them both to relive the nightmare of losing their siblings.

"I'm game!" Caydence ripped her long T-shirt off, revealing her red bikini, and then she dived into the water. Zane was right behind her, the two of them vanishing under the water that had replaced her hardwood floor.

"This isn't the best place for swimming," Jeremiah said with a scowl. "We should really move over to the cove so that—"

A wave rocked the boat, sending Carly over the side.

"Carly!" Jeremiah called, but that was the last thing she heard before the sound of fiberglass crashing into fiberglass consumed her world. Carly was pulled under when her shirt was caught on debris. Panic set in, but somehow, she managed to free herself from her shirt and popped back up to the surface. It was at that moment when everything slowed down. Jeremiah was swimming away from her, calling for Zane. He was frantic and almost to Zane's side when his brother was suddenly pulled under. Jeremiah dived down into the water, but when he resurfaced, he was sputtering about Zane vanishing.

"He has to be there. I just saw him." Jeremiah disappeared beneath the surface again.

Carly knew that's when she'd spotted her sister floating facedown in the water. Her heart had shattered into a million pieces when she realized she was already gone. From that moment on, everything had been a blur. But in the memory, her gaze was fixated on where Zane had disappeared beneath the surface, and something reflecting off the water caught her eye. It was another boat, speeding away from them. And Carly could've sworn she'd heard Zane cry out, "Go back! They need help."

The vision vanished, and suddenly Carly was sitting on her hardwood floor in her herb studio, shaking like a leaf, her adrenaline rush fading.

"Carly?" Jeremiah asked, his voice gruff and full of emotion.

"Yeah?" She lifted her gaze to his, finding his face drained of color.

"That accident wasn't an accident at all," he said.

This time it was Carly's eyes that widened. "What? Are you sure?"

He nodded. "That boat didn't even try to turn. In the vision, I watched it plow right into us, swing around and circle us, and then speed off across the bay."

"With Zane," she added, her chest tight and her eyes filled with tears. "They did it on purpose and then grabbed Zane out of the water and took him with them."

Jeremiah let out a gasp. "Are you sure?"

"About ninety percent sure. I swear I heard him demanding that they come back for us."

"But why?" he asked. "I can't think of any reason why someone would try to sink our boat and then take Zane. Was he into anything shady that I didn't know about?"

Carly shook her head. "No. I can't think of anything. But that vision... Everything else was exactly as I remember it. I don't know why the added details would be different."

"That means... Zane is alive."

"And we have to find him. One way or another, we need to bring him home," Carly finished for him.

Jeremiah took two steps, pulled Carly into a hug, and held on tightly, crushing her to him.

There was silence as they each held on. Carly had known that remembering that day would be hard, but she hadn't imagined that they'd actually relive it. The experience had been brutal. How was she supposed to process reliving the death of her twin sister?

Tears spilled unchecked down her cheeks and her body racked with sobs as she let herself grieve.

Jeremiah didn't say a word. He knew all too well that there was nothing to say that could make any of it better. All he did was hold her close and run his hand over her head, soothing her. When her tears finally stopped, he dropped a soft kiss on the top of her head and let her go. "I can't imagine what it's been like for you without Caydence here all these years."

"It's like half of myself is missing," she admitted. Then she told him something she'd never told another person. "I think it's why I like acting so much. It gives me a chance to be someone else. Someone who isn't missing half her heart." His anguished eyes were too much to bear. She glanced away. "There's no hope of bringing her back. I know that. But it doesn't mean I don't wish things were different."

"I know," he said.

Carly wiped at her eyes and straightened her spine. "But this isn't about Caydence. It's about Zane. And now that we have another reason to believe that he's alive, we need to figure out how to find him and bring him home."

Jeremiah held the compass out to her, but instead of taking it, she clasped her hand over his and said, "We'll bring him back to both of us."

CHAPTER SIX

*C*arly sat at her table sipping a mug of coffee in the late afternoon as she thought of her evening the night before with Jeremiah. The vision they'd shared had connected them in a way that she'd only ever experienced with her sister. It was that shared bond that came from an experience that only the two of them understood. The feeling both comforted her and frightened her a little. She was so used to being on her own for the past three decades that she wasn't sure how to process such a feeling.

Still, she couldn't deny that she wanted that connection. Had even craved it over the years.

"You look serious," Harlow said as she wandered into the kitchen wearing yoga pants and a sweatshirt. She'd just come back from a class and looked more relaxed than Carly had seen her in weeks. Harlow stopped in front of her aunt. "What have you done to your hair?"

"Is it a rat's nest?" Carly asked as she raised her hand to run it over her head. She'd tied her mass of curls up into a pony tail when she'd rolled out of bed only an hour ago, but hadn't taken the time to comb it out first. Her time clock was a complete mess after her all-nighter at the hospital.

"No, it's..." Harlow bit her lip. "I mean, it's a choice, but it isn't what I would've chosen. Not yet anyway. I'd have given you a few more decades before you decided to go with the natural look."

"What are you talking about?" Carly got up and moved toward the hall bathroom.

"I know silver hair is a thing right now, but I think you're going to need to dye it so that it's all the same color of gray," Harlow added as she followed her.

"Gray?!" Carly hurried into the bathroom, panicked. She'd just had her hair done a couple weeks ago. Surely her roots weren't showing already. Besides, even though she was in her early fifties, only a few areas around her face had started to go gray, and most of those blended in with her blond hair. She came to an abrupt stop in front of her mirror, and her eyes widened in horror as she let out a shriek. Her honey blond hair had turned various shades of gray overnight, and to top it off, one long gray whisker had sprouted on her chin.

"I look like a crypt keeper!" Carly turned her head from side to side and nearly cried at her appearance. Had she aged twenty years overnight? And what was up with that chin whisker? "Call Rebekah. This is a beauty emergency."

"Um, so you weren't trying for gray?" Harlow asked, sounding confused.

"Of course not! Do you really think I'd do this on purpose?"

"I thought it was a dye job gone bad. I mean, the last time I saw you, your hair was a gorgeous shade of blond," Harlow said. "I don't get it."

"Neither do I." Carly hurried past her niece and ran for her master bathroom where she kept her trusty tweezers. And when she looked into her magnifying mirror, her horror continued. Fine lines that hadn't been there before branched from her lips. The few that had been around her eyes had multiplied. It felt as if she was watching herself age with each second that went by. Carly's voice shook as she said, "Harlow?"

"What is it?" Harlow moved to stand right beside her.

"I need an anti-aging potion ASAP. Call Gigi. It's an emergency."

Harlow scanned Carly's face and the same horror that had seized Carly was written all over her expression. She must've finally taken a good look at what was happening.

"Now," Carly demanded.

"Right." Her niece spun on her heel and ran out of the bathroom.

Carly hurried into her herb studio and opened her big reference book. Her heart was thundering against her chest, and everything started to ache. Exhausted, she sat on her stool and tried to read the glossary. Only the words swam in her vision and it was nearly impossible to read anything. "Dammit!" She rummaged around in her drawer, looking for a pair of readers, hoping that some eye correction would help her make sense of the reference book. Once she had the glasses on, she squinted at the book. The letters had stopped floating, but they were still blurry until she pushed the book farther away. Suddenly, everything came into focus, and she flipped to the section on anti-aging herbs.

There it was, exactly what she needed: Basil, cinnamon, clove, ginger, and a handful of other herbs. She quickly moved to her jars of dried herbs and made a hasty concoction with a warm coconut water she'd left on her bench. The herb solution tasted like dirt, but she choked it down even as she nearly gagged.

"Gigi is on her way," Harlow said as she rushed into the studio. "Carly! Ohmigod!"

Carly turned to her, but she moved too fast and nearly lost her balance. If it hadn't been for the workbench to grab onto, she'd have fallen to the floor in a heap of bones. She glanced down at her hands that were clutching the bench and let out a cry of distress. "I'm shrinking into nothing!"

Harlow was by her side instantly. "Come on, Auntie. Let's get you to the couch."

Carly didn't resist. What else was there to do? She'd already tried to combat the problem with a potion. It clearly hadn't worked. At the rate she was aging, if she didn't sit down, she'd likely break a hip. Tears stung her eyes, but she blinked them back. Gigi was on her way. Together, they'd find a way to save her from wasting away into oblivion.

Once she was settled on the couch, Harlow tucked a blanket around her and ordered her to stay there while she made some tea. Carly closed her eyes and nodded, trying to put the horror of what was happening to her out of her mind.

"Carly?" Harlow said, shaking her shoulder.

She startled and blinked up at her niece who was holding a cup of tea. "Did I fall asleep?"

Harlow nodded and handed her the cup. Then she grabbed a scone from a tray on the coffee table and pressed it into Carly's free hand. "Eat this. The sugar should help."

Exhaustion weighed down Carly's limbs, but she sipped at the tea and took a bite of the scone. The pastry was like cardboard in her mouth, but she forced it down, knowing that was no fault of the scone. She'd had one the night before, and it had been delicious.

"That's it," Harlow said, smoothing her hair. "Eat a little more."

Carly felt like her limbs were made of lead, but she did as she was told, if only so she could keep her focus on something other than her rapid aging. After a few more sips of tea, her eyes closed again, and she didn't remember anything until she heard Gigi's voice.

"Help me tilt her head back. She needs to swallow this as soon as possible." There was an urgency to Gigi's tone that startled Carly awake.

"Am I dead?" Carly asked, blinking up at the woman who was hovering over her.

"No, thank the goddess," Gigi said, relief clear in her amber eyes. "Can you sit up a little? I need you to drink this entire potion. Can you do that?"

Carly's voice was wobbly as she said, "Of course." But when she went to push herself into a sitting position, she had trouble keeping herself upright.

"I've got you," Gigi said, holding her shoulders so she didn't slump over.

Using both her hands, Carly held the thermos up to her lips and started to drink. "Ugh!" she sputtered when the bitter potion hit her tongue. "What's in this?"

"Tree bark and a bunch of other stuff. I'll tell you after you choke it down."

Carly grimaced but tilted the thermos up and slowly started to drink the horrendous potion. With each sip, her strength slowly started to return and after a minute, she was able to gulp the potion down, barely tasting it as she consumed the last drop.

"Thank the goddess." Gigi sat down next to her and slumped her shoulders in relief.

"It worked!" Harlow threw her arms around Gigi. "Thank

you so much. I swear if you'd taken even ten more minutes, I was certain she was going to disappear right before my eyes."

Gigi squeezed Harlow's hand. "It's unlikely that would've happened, but I can see why you thought that." She turned to Carly. "How much magic have you cast in the last twenty-four hours?"

"Well..." Carly stared at her hands, relieved they were no longer wrinkled and shriveling by the second. "I made a potion to stimulate memory, and then I cast a spell so that Jeremiah and I could remember our siblings."

Gigi groaned. "A memory spell? For two people?"

"Yes. Why? Is that bad?" Carly asked, confused. She'd found the spell in a standard text. It hadn't come with any warnings.

"It is if you don't cast a protection ring." Gigi took Carly's hand in hers. "That spell could've killed you," she said in a hushed whisper. "Do me a favor, and from now on only do those kinds of spells with the rest of the coven, okay? It's safer in numbers, and we can provide a protection ring."

"Uh, sure," Carly said. "But I don't want to inconvenience you and your friends."

"Carly," Gigi said with an exaggerated sigh. "*You* are our friend."

"But I'm not officially part of the coven," Carly insisted. "I don't want to be a burden."

"You're not," Gigi said with her hands on her hips, her voice stern. "We all love you and consider you one of us. Now get up off that couch and get me something with alcohol in it. I need it after throwing together that reversal potion."

"Right." Carly got up, half expecting herself to collapse from the effort, but to her relief she was as strong as ever and even had a burst of energy as if she'd woken up refreshed after a power nap.

The other two women followed her into her kitchen and sat at the counter, watching her every move.

"I can't believe the difference," Harlow said, turning to Gigi. "That potion of yours is a damned miracle."

Gigi grinned at her. "Even I'm impressed it worked so well."

"Ouch!" Carly dropped the empty glass she'd just picked up by her fingertips and clutched her wrist. "Son of a... Dammit, that hurts."

"What did you do?" Harlow asked, jumping up and running over to her aunt, inspecting her as if she was the one who'd just broken into a hundred pieces instead of the glass that shattered on her floor.

"I just pulled something in my wrist when I picked up that glass." Carly turned to Gigi. "Is your potion wearing off?"

Gigi studied her a moment, but then shook her head. "No. Everything else about you is perfectly normal. I think what happened is you just pulled a fifty."

"A fifty?" Carly asked, frowning at her in confusion as Harlow laughed and went to work cleaning up the broken glass.

"You know, when your body gives out for no other reason than your age?" Gigi winked at her. "Like when you throw your back out when you sneeze or roll over in bed. Pretty sure your wrist injury is the same thing."

Carly scowled. "Well that blows. And here I was thinking I'd just gotten a shot of energy from your potion."

Gigi nodded. "Yep. Overconfidence. It'll get you every time." She chuckled as she filled a bag of ice and then handed it to Carly. "Here, use this until it's numb or until the alcohol kicks in."

"If this pulling a fifty thing keeps up, I might turn into an alcoholic," Carly said as she grabbed another glass and held it out until Gigi filled it and two others with the aged bourbon she'd grabbed from her cupboard.

"Cheers," Gigi said, clinking her glass to Carly's. "Welcome back to the age where things just start falling apart for no reason."

Carly rolled her shoulders and flexed her fingers, trying to ease the tension in her wrist. "It's better than the alternative, right?"

"Amen, sister." Gigi downed her glass of amber liquid and was ready with the bottle when Carly did the same.

"It's five o'clock somewhere, right?" Carly said with a laugh and decided after the last few days, she deserved to get toasted with Gigi and her niece.

CHAPTER SEVEN

"What have I done?" Carly groaned when she tried to pry her eyes open the next morning. Was that a woodpecker hammering at her brain from the inside of her skull? The sun glinted off the Pacific and through her window, blinding her. "Ugh. Someone put me out of my misery."

There was a soft chuckle followed by the weight of someone sitting on her mattress. "Gigi said to drink this when you wake up. She thought you'd need it," Harlow said, sounding entirely too perky for someone who helped her clean out her liquor cabinet the night before.

"No." Carly rolled over and covered her head with one of her pillows. "Let me die in peace."

"You'll feel better. I promise."

Carly lifted the pillow slightly. "Or I'll end up shrinking two inches and needing a walker to get around the house."

Harlow snorted. "Now you're just being dramatic. Sit up and drink your potion before Joy gets here."

"Joy's coming over?" Carly frowned and winced at the pain from moving her face muscles.

"Yes," Harlow said with a sigh. "Don't you remember? You and Gigi made plans to meet the coven at the bluff to try a finding spell. But when you guys called Joy, she said she wanted to come by first to try to elicit a vision of Zane. If she can, it would prove he's still alive."

That got Carly sitting up and downing the potion that Harlow held out to her. It had a faint floral scent that made her queasy. For a moment, she thought she was going to lose the contents of her stomach, but she took a deep breath and was able to hold it together. "I don't think this helped," Carly said.

"Your complexion is a slightly less vile shade of green. Give it a second." Harlow patted her arm and moved to the door. "I'm going out with Lex today. Try to keep the alcohol poisoning to a minimum today, okay? I rather like having you around."

"You just like my beach house," Carly said, holding her head and willing the pounding to stop.

Harlow shook her head at her aunt. "I'm your heir. I get to keep the view either way. I'd rather it be with you around."

"Right. I forgot. The booze fried my brain," Carly said, rubbing a temple. "But don't worry. More booze is the last thing on the agenda for today."

"Good to hear. I'd get in the shower if I were you," Harlow said and wrinkled her nose. "At this point it's probably the booze stench radiating off of you that's making your stomach turn. Besides, you don't want to look like you crawled out from underneath a table at some dive bar when Joy gets here, do you?"

"No." Carly pushed herself up and then asked, "You're going out with Lex?"

"Yep." She waved and disappeared down the hall.

Carly briefly wondered when Harlow had become friends with Grace's niece. They knew each other, of course. Premonition Pointe just wasn't that big of a town. But she hadn't realized that the two had started seeing each other socially. The knowledge made Carly happy. Harlow needed more people in her life other than just her aunt. Lex was a nice person. She was glad they were becoming friends.

Carly took her niece's advice and headed into her oversized bathroom to transform into a more human version of herself. One that didn't smell like a distillery.

* * *

"THERE YOU ARE!" Joy called as she stepped out onto Carly's deck. "When you didn't answer the front door, I figured I'd find you out here."

Carly waved her over where she was laying in the sun, trying to soak up the warmth of the rays. After she'd showered and managed to put herself back together, she'd grabbed another cup of coffee and headed out to listen to the surf. The ocean always seemed to soothe her nerves. And she'd needed it. Her entire body had practically been buzzing with anxiety. She couldn't stop thinking about what they would do if the finding spell didn't work.

"I never get tired of this view," Joy said, sitting in the chair next to Carly. "Ever since I moved in with Troy, I have to force myself away from the windows so that I don't waste an entire day just mesmerized by the crashing waves. Though it is infinitely more enjoyable than listening to Kira, my latest costar, complain about her acne or the boy who hasn't asked her out yet."

Carly snorted. "She has to be better than Prissy Penderton." Prissy was the actress who'd played Joy's daughter in the first movie they'd done together. "That girl was the worst."

Joy shuddered. "You couldn't pay me enough to work with her again. You're right. I'd rather listen to all the junior high gossip Kira can dish out than deal with Prissy again. Next thing you know, I'm going to be hosting a pajama party and leading a Ouija Board session."

"Do those work?" Carly asked, sitting up in her chair. "I always wondered."

"How would I know?" Joy laughed. "I spent twenty-five years raising my kids and trying to make a failing marriage work. Maybe we should try it. Although, Hope or Gigi would be the ones to ask. Gigi talks to ghosts and Hope is the type to try anything once."

Carly smiled at her. "We'll ask them first. Spells and potions are one thing, but using some board to conjure up random ghosts? That's entirely another."

"What if the ghosts aren't random?" Joy asked with a raised eyebrow.

"You mean like my sister or… Zane?" Carly forced his name out. Now that there was reason to hope that her old friend was alive, she'd started to believe that they'd find him. She knew it was stupid to get her hopes up, but she couldn't help it.

"I didn't mean Zane," Joy said, giving Carly a pained look. "I meant your sister. You must miss her."

"I do," Carly said with a nod. "But she already visits me. I don't need a Ouija Board to talk to her."

"She does?" Joy's eyes widened. "Now that's interesting. I bet you could make that Ouija Board planchette move without even touching it."

"Not according to the scientists," Carly quipped. "They all

believe it's just unconscious muscle movement. I doubt that's the case for witches, but I've never tried. I've been working under the impression that those who want to speak with us will come on their own."

"Yeah. That makes sense," Joy said. "I was just thinking…" She shook her head. "Never mind."

"You were thinking that if we called Zane and he showed up, then we'd know, right?" Carly asked.

Joy slowly nodded. "I know that's not the outcome you want. It's better to stay positive."

"It's not that I'm afraid that he'll show up," Carly said, frowning. "Not at all. As much as I want him to be alive, if he's not, then it's better that we know. I just don't believe that he would show himself. I've asked my sister Caydence about him when she shows herself to me. More than a few times. She says she hasn't seen him since the day of the accident. She speculated that he moved on. But now…"

"Now you think he's still with us," Joy answered and squeezed her hand.

Carly nodded. "In my heart, I truly do."

"Then let's see if we can find him. Do you have a picture of him? I'm ready to try to get a vision of him."

"Yeah." Carly jumped up out of her chair and had to steady herself for a moment. The potion Harlow made her drink had worked. She no longer thought she was going to vomit up her internal organs, but she was still tired and on the weak side.

"You okay?" Joy asked, steadying her.

"Yeah, just feeling my age. I swear, I should've stopped drinking altogether the moment I turned fifty."

Joy let out a small gasp. "Give up drinking? Have you lost your mind? What about margarita night? Or mimosas? Or heck, what about all the wine in my wine rack?"

Carly couldn't help chuckling. "Don't worry. I didn't mean it. But I definitely think I'm going to try not to get so drunk that I'm missing random chunks of time. Plus, the hangover is a bitch."

"I bet." Joy grinned at her. "Had a wild night, huh?"

"Gigi got me toasted. We'll blame her."

Laughing, Joy gestured to the house. "Should we go in and get started?"

Carly led her into the house and over to her dining room table. She'd already laid out a picture of Zane. It was actually one of him and Jeremiah. It had been taken on the day she and Zane had graduated high school. The same day Zane had decided to move to LA with her so they could both start looking for acting jobs. She had never been happier to know that her bestie would be by her side.

"This is Zane?" Joy asked, pointing to the correct brother.

Carly nodded.

She squinted at the picture. "Jeremiah certainly was handsome back then, wasn't he?"

"Yeah," Carly said, averting her gaze so the other woman wouldn't know how much thinking about him affected her.

"But he's much more distinguished now." Joy's tone was matter-of-fact when she added, "Isn't it crazy how some men can just keep getting better looking without much effort, while us women spend a fortune to maintain our beauty standards?"

Carly couldn't help the bark of laughter that burst from her lips. She hadn't been expecting Joy to contemplate the beauty standards of men and women. Joy wasn't wrong though. Jeremiah had only improved with age. Which was impressive since he'd always been beautiful. "It's completely unfair," Carly agreed.

Joy smirked at her. "Zane has the same genes. No doubt

that if he is alive he probably has women following him around."

"Perhaps. But they'd be wasting their time. He's gay." Carly gave Joy a sad smile. "Unless he's forgotten that, too."

"I doubt that's something one forgets," Joy said and reached across the table to squeeze Carly's hand. "I also have a very hard time believing that he'd stay away from you if he had any choice in the matter."

Carly nodded. "Thanks."

Joy stared at the picture for what seemed like hours, though it was likely only a few minutes. Carly was certain that the vision wasn't working, and that Joy was just giving it time before she gave up. But just as Carly was about to thank her for trying, Joy's head snapped up and her gaze turned unfocused. Her mouth dropped open.

Carly stared at her with wide eyes. She'd witnessed Joy have visions before, but she'd never looked like she'd snapped into a trance. As if she were possessed by some unknown force. The times it had happened before, Joy had just looked like she was focused on the picture and lost in some sort of memory. This was… different. More intense. And if Carly was honest, a lot intimidating.

The house was so silent that Carly could hear the clock on the far wall. *Tick. Tick. Tick.* Joy sat at the table, stock-still, her chest rising with each breath she took. Carly focused on her, willing her to come out of the trance. To have her confirm that she saw Zane and knew exactly where to start looking for him.

Joy sucked in a sharp breath and jerked her gaze to Carly.

Carly's heart raced, and she reached across the table to squeeze Joy's hand. "You saw him?"

Her friend shook her head slowly as fear crept into her eyes. "Not Zane. Jeremiah."

Carly's entire body turned ice cold. "What is it? What did you see?"

"Someone is tracking him. I saw…" She shook her head and grimaced. "I'm not sure exactly what I saw."

"Just tell me whatever it was," Carly said carefully, trying to force her voice to remain steady. Clearly, whatever Joy saw had spooked her. "We'll figure it out." They'd have to. Because if Jeremiah was in danger, Carly would stop at nothing to keep him safe. "Joy?"

"Oh, man. I'm sorry. I'm not trying to freak you out. It's just that the vision was so clear and yet so confusing at the same time."

"I don't understand," Carly said. "What does that mean?"

Joy stood and started to pace the kitchen. "Jeremiah was leaving the Sea Pointe Inn. He had his head down and wasn't looking up when a man in jeans and a blue button-down shirt rounded the corner and started to follow him. He had the look of a repair man and drove a nondescript white van."

"You mean this person was following Jeremiah in a white van?" Carly asked as she pressed her hand to her aching chest. An alarm bell was going off in her head. Jeremiah was in danger.

Joy nodded and clutched the back of her chair until her knuckles turned white. "The white van followed Jeremiah and swerved out into an oncoming lane, appearing to want to pass him. But then the van jerked to the right, forcing Jeremiah to swerve right onto a country road. The van tried to follow him, but another car cut him off, causing a fender bender. Before anyone could get out to survey the damage, the white van took off."

"We have to do something," Carly said, reaching for her keys on a side table. "We need to warn Jeremiah." She strode toward her garage, intending to find Jeremiah immediately to let him know that he could be in danger due to his efforts to find his brother.

"Carly?" Joy called, running across the kitchen to keep up with her.

"We need to go, Joy. Come on."

"But can't you try calling him first? Make sure he's okay and warn him before this happens again?"

"Right." Carly paused, taking a moment to let herself calm down. She hadn't been thinking clearly. Where would she even go to warn Jeremiah? The inn? She had no idea if he was even there. She fished out her phone and dialed. Voicemail. "Jeremiah, it's Carly. I need you to call me as soon as you get this message. Joy had a vision. Someone is following you. Be careful. Please."

Joy squeezed Carly's hand. "I'm sorry I didn't see Zane."

Carly shook her head. "No need to apologize. I'm just glad you saw the person following Jeremiah before something terrible happened to him, too." She gestured to the door. "Can we go by the inn on the way to meet the coven? I want to see if we can catch him there."

"Of course." Joy followed Carly into the garage and slid into the passenger seat of her car. "He's fine. You know that, right?"

Carly nodded, but in her gut, all she felt was dread.

CHAPTER EIGHT

*J*eremiah wasn't at the inn or at the hospital where John Doe was still unconscious. The bodyguard from Carly's security team who was watching over him said he hadn't seen Jeremiah that morning. With no other ideas of where to look for him, Carly finally pointed her car toward the bluff where she and Joy were to meet the rest of the coven.

"I'm sure he got your message," Joy said.

Carly glanced at her. "We don't know that. Not until he calls me back."

"Right." Joy chewed on her bottom lip. "I wish there was something more I could do."

"I know. But thanks to you, we now know that someone is following Jeremiah. Maybe it's the same person who attacked our John Doe." Carly hated that thought, but it seemed to be the only plausible explanation. She glanced in her rearview mirror, and relief flooded through her when she spotted Jake keeping pace behind her in his SUV. It had taken her a long time to get used to the idea that she might need security around to watch out for her, but after her niece was taken from her home, there hadn't been any other choice. She didn't mind, really. Her team did a great job of giving her space while also making sure she was protected. And now she was just grateful. If someone was following Jeremiah, how long would it be before they started tailing her?

"If they wanted to kill John Doe, it makes sense they wouldn't want anyone around to talk to him when he wakes up," Joy agreed. "That's not good news for us though, is it?"

Carly jerked her attention to her friend, horror filling her. "You're right. This means you and the rest of the coven have to stay away from this. I can't ask you all to put yourselves in danger."

Joy scoffed. "Please. Just try to make us stay away. Have you even met us? Remember what happened when Iris needed our help? We ended up taking down a criminal ring that was intent on destroying Premonition Pointe."

That was true. Because of the new mayor and his cronies, the entire town had been cursed and it affected everyone. But if Carly let them get involved in finding Zane, it could put all of them in danger and none of them had security following them around. "It's not safe."

"It's not safe having some stranger running around shooting people in Premonition Pointe either, Carly," Joy said, her tone firm. "You can't stop us. You can try, but it won't work."

"But—" Carly started, determined to try and talk some sense into her.

Joy put her hand up, stopping her. "This is a losing battle. But you don't have to take my word for it. We'll ask the rest of the coven what they think."

Carly sighed. She wasn't used to not getting her way. But

more importantly, she wasn't used to people sticking their necks out for her. As much as she wanted to yell at Joy to not get involved so she'd stay out of danger, she was also deeply touched. "Thank you."

Joy's lips twitched into a ghost of a smile. "For what? Snapping at you?"

"For being a great friend." Carly smiled, but her eyes misted with emotion, and she had to turn away before she turned into a blubbering idiot.

"You're a great friend, too. You know that, right?" Joy asked. Her tone was hesitant, as if she wasn't sure Carly would believe her.

The truth was Carly knew she was a gracious hostess and coworker. But friends had been in short supply for a long time. She wasn't actually sure if she knew how to be a great friend anymore.

"Carly, seriously. You know that, right?" Joy demanded.

Carly shook her head. "No. But I'm working on it." Damn, now she just sounded pathetic. Her phone rang through her car audio system, and Jeremiah's name flashed on the screen. She instantly accepted the call. "Jeremiah! Where are you?"

"I'm at the autobody shop getting a dent pulled out of my fender. I just got your message. You think I'm being followed?"

"Yes," Joy said before Carly answered. "Hi, Jeremiah. It's Joy here. I touched a photo of you and had a vision in real time. I saw the van that tried to run you off the road and likely caused the dent in your fender. The driver was dressed like some kind of service repair person and followed you when you left the inn. If it hadn't been for another car nearly running him off the road, I fear he'd have done much worse. You need to be careful and probably report this incident to the police."

"Uh. Okay," he said. "Someone really followed me?"

"Yes," Carly confirmed. "Sorry, we're in the car. That's why you're on speaker. We think the guy who followed you had something to do with the shooting outside my house. He probably doesn't like us hanging around waiting for his victim to wake up."

Jeremiah swore and then cleared his throat. "I guess that makes sense. I can't think of a reason why anyone else would be trying to run me off the road."

There was silence over the line until Carly couldn't take it anymore and then said, "I suppose it's possible he was blinded by your good looks and just lost control of his vehicle."

Joy snorted.

Jeremiah let out a sigh, and Carly could've sworn she actually heard him roll his eyes.

"Oh, come on. There's nothing wrong with gallows humor," Carly said.

That got a chuckle out of him. "You always did have your dark side."

"Listen," Carly said, forcing confidence into her tone. "I think you should stay at my house while you're in town."

"What? No, Carly. I don't think—"

"Jeremiah," Carly said, cutting him off. "Someone just tried to run you off the road. If the person who tried to kill John Doe is trying to hurt you or at least scare you enough to stay away, then wouldn't it make sense to stay where there is some security? Because we both know that neither of us are going to let this go until we know for sure if Zane is alive."

"I could hire my own security," he said, but he sounded like he was talking more to himself than Carly.

"You could. But then we'd have two cars following us around. That won't be conspicuous at all." The sarcasm dripped off her tongue.

Jeremiah sighed in defeat. "All right. You have a point. After I'm done here with the car, I'll head to your place. Sound good?"

"Yes. And go ahead and check out of the inn. There's plenty of space at my house for as long as you need." Carly turned into the street that led to the bluff where they were meeting the coven. Three cars were already lined up along the road. She pulled in behind the last one and killed the engine. "Jeremiah?" she prompted when she realized he hadn't answered her.

"I'm here," he said. "I just don't want to put you out. You know what they say about company and bad fish smelling after three days."

"It's been over thirty years since we've seen each other. Surely we can take this time to get to know each other again. Right?"

"Sure. Yeah. You're right," he said, though he still sounded hesitant.

She couldn't blame him. She probably wouldn't be comfortable staying in his house either. Warmth settled in her chest at the thought, and she wondered if it was true that she'd feel uneasy being his houseguest. Maybe not. This was Jeremiah after all, the first man she'd ever been half in love with. Perhaps she'd actually love to stay with him indefinitely. Carly shook her head, trying to dislodge her thoughts. Now was not the time to moon over her unrequited crush from her youth.

"So it's settled then," she said, leaving no room for argument. "I'm meeting with the coven today. We're trying a finding spell. I'll call you as soon as we know anything."

Jeremiah let out a whoosh of air. "Thank you. And thank the coven members for me, too."

"Will do." Carly ended the call, and when she glanced over at Joy, the other woman was eyeing her with a sly grin. "What?"

"You have a major crush on him," Joy said, her tone teasing.

"No, I don't." Carly rolled her eyes and climbed out of the car.

Joy followed and tucked her bag over her shoulder as she rushed to keep up with Carly, who was striding across the bluff. "I think you definitely have some feelings for that guy. Not that I blame you. He's seriously sexy."

"You think so?" Carly asked before she could stop herself.

"Um, yeah. It's really not even debatable. You *had* to have noticed that thick dark hair and that intense gaze of his. It's enough to make a girl curl her toes just looking at him." Joy fanned herself playfully.

Carly raised a questioning eyebrow. "Sounds like you're the one with some feelings for the guy."

Joy chuckled. "Nah. Troy is plenty for me, but I'm not blind. The man is undeniably gorgeous. But it's more than that for you, isn't it?"

"I don't…" Carly sighed. "He's just an old friend who I haven't been in touch with for a very long time. I'm just trying to figure out where we stand. Did I have a crush on him when we were younger? Sure. But now?" Carly lifted her shoulders and hands palms up in unison. "I barely know him, and we're both invested in finding Zane. There's no room for indulging in crushes or thinking about romance. All I want is for Jeremiah to stay safe and for us to find Zane."

Joy reached over and squeezed her hand. "I know. I'm sorry for teasing you. I just thought it would lighten the mood a bit."

Carly gave her a grateful smile while also mentally kicking herself. Clearly, Joy had hit a nerve since Carly had overreacted to her comments. She told herself to relax and said, "You're right that he's gorgeous. And having him stay at my house won't exactly be a hardship on the eyes."

"That's the spirit." Joy winked at her and then linked her arm through Carly's as they made their way to the rest of the coven who'd already formed a magical circle with salt and pillar candles.

"Thank you all for coming," Carly said as she glanced around at her friends. Grace, Hope, Iris, and Gigi all stood, and each came over to hug Carly. They murmured their support and promised to do whatever they could to help her find her childhood friend. Carly blinked back her tears of gratitude and hugged each one of them. "You have no idea what this means to me."

"Oh, I think we do," Gigi said, reaching out and engulfing Carly's free hand with her own. "All of us have been in situations where we needed the help of our coven sisters. We're more than happy to pay the favor forward."

The rest of the coven nodded their agreement, and Carly smiled gratefully at them while making a promise to herself to stop being surprised by the friendship she'd found in these women. "Okay then. We're all here. What do we need to do to get started?"

"Join the circle," Grace said as she stepped behind one of the pillar candles. The rest of the women fell into place, leaving the space across from Grace free for Carly.

Once she was in place, Carly instantly felt her skin start to tingle with magic. She stared down at her arms and let out a small gasp when her skin started to glow.

"It's powerful, isn't it?" Joy said. "It's the collective energy already flowing through us."

"But we didn't even do anything yet," Carly marveled. She'd helped the coven do a finding spell once before, but she hadn't felt anything close to what she was feeling that day. It was as if something had opened up in her and she was finally able to give all of herself to the coven.

"That's what happens when you hook up with a handful of badass witches," Hope said with a wink. She pushed a dark curl out of her eyes and raised her hands to the sky, seemingly soaking in the power that crackled around them.

Gigi mimicked her stance and swayed in the breeze.

One by one the rest lifted their hands to the sky and tilted their faces to the sun. Carly followed and felt as if she were being filled up with the energy of not only the sun, but the rest of the women gathered around her.

"Carly," Iris said. "This is your show. You're the one who has the connection to Zane. Did you bring something of his?"

"I did." Carly retrieved the compass Zane had given her from her pocket. She'd tried to return it to Jeremiah, but he'd refused, insisting that if Zane had given it to her, then that was where it belonged.

"Do you remember what to do?" Gigi asked her. The gorgeous woman was wearing a white dress that was blowing in the wind, and Carly couldn't help but think of her as some sort of goddess. She had that ethereal look about her.

Carly cleared her throat. "Yes. I think so."

"Good. We're ready when you are," Gigi said.

Holding the compass tightly in one hand, Carly cleared her mind and focused on Zane. She pictured him sitting on the fallen log in the woods beneath the aging treehouse behind his childhood home. It was where they usually met when they wanted to hang out without the watchful eye of his parents or her grandmother. They'd spent a lot of time there, talking about their futures. It was also where they'd planned their lives after high school and where she'd begged him to go to LA with her. It was always the place she pictured him when she indulged in her memories.

Gigi pressed a handful of herbs into her palm. "Toss these into the fire when you start your incantation."

Carly nodded to indicate she understood, but she didn't open her eyes. She was already fixated on the memory of Zane and didn't want to let it go.

The other witches started a low chant, inviting the fire to ignite.

It wasn't long before Carly heard the whoosh of the magical fire and felt the warmth of the flames emanating from the center of the circle.

"Now, Carly," Gigi said softly.

"Goddess of the Earth, we seek one of my heart. Show him to us, let us know that he is not lost." The incantation was modified from the one they'd used before when Iris had been searching for Kade. Carly had wanted it to be more personalized, because she believed the intention behind incantations were more important than the specific words. No one on that bluff knew or cared for Zane more than she did.

Carly repeated the incantation, her voice stronger and steadier than before. And when she felt a bolt of power seize her, she tossed the herbs Gigi had given her into the fire, making it roar. Her eyes popped open, and suddenly Carly was fixated on the six-foot-high flames. They twisted and curled on each other, turning white and then blue as the blaze burned hotter.

One of the other witches let out a gasp, but Carly couldn't tear her eyes away from the fire. The flames started to separate, and suddenly the outline of a tall, lanky person appeared. She squinted, trying to make out any features, but the person's face wasn't clearly defined. She wanted to scream with frustration. There was no way to know if the person reflected within the blaze was Zane or— Then the person started to walk and just like that, she knew.

"Zane," she whispered as she eyed the awkward gait she'd know anywhere. Zane had experienced a rapid growth spurt of about six inches in a year that had left him with pain in his left hip. After therapy, the pain had resolved, but the unusual gait he'd used to compensate hadn't ever fully normalized.

"Where is he, Carly? Where is Zane?" The voice behind her sounded like Jeremiah's. But that couldn't be right. He wasn't at the bluff. Was he?

The scene shifted, and she watched as Zane sat in a room poring over some sort of old school ledger in a notebook. He rubbed at his eyes and then looked up. His eyes widened as he stared directly at Carly. There was recognition in his gaze.

"Zane," Carly said again, only louder, trying to make sure he heard her.

Zane's brow furrowed and he looked confused for a moment before he shook his head and blinked as if to clear his vision. Then he lowered his head and continued to study the ledger.

"No! Zane, look at me. It's me, Carly!" she cried.

Her old friend jerked his head up, his eyes searching. After a few moments, he ran a hand through his dark hair and clutched at it in frustration.

"I'm here. We're looking for you. If you could just tell me where you are, we'll come for you. I promise. Me and Jeremiah. We're waiting for you."

She watched him mouth the name *Jeremiah*.

"I know you can hear me," she said excitedly. "Please, Zane. Help us out. Tell us where to find you and we'll be there as soon as possible."

"Jeremiah," Zane said again, his eyes still frantically searching for her... or maybe for Jeremiah.

"He's looking for you," Carly tried. "He won't give up until you're home."

"Home?" His confusion cleared, and once again he was staring right into Carly's eyes. "I don't know where home is."

Carly's heart nearly broke in two. Her suspicions were confirmed. He'd either been spelled or he had amnesia. She knew there was a reason they'd never heard from him. "We'll help you remember, Zane. I promise. Just lead us to where you are now, and we won't stop until you're safely back with your family." She held the compass up, praying he could see it.

He blinked twice, and then in an astonished voice he said, "Carly? Is it really you?"

Tears sprang to her eyes as she nodded. "It's really me. I miss you."

"I miss you, too," he choked out over a sob.

Carly reached out with her free hand, trying to connect with him.

He did the same, but their hands never did touch. Still, they both held them there as if they'd made a physical connection.

"Where are you, Zane?" Carly asked again, desperate to get his location. Now that she knew for sure he was still alive, she'd move heaven and earth to bring him back to both her and Jeremiah.

"I..." He jerked and glanced around as if he'd been startled. When he met her gaze again, he whispered, "Enchantment."

The flames came together, cutting off her window into Zane's world right before the fire extinguished altogether, leaving her staring at the charred remains of the logs in the middle of the circle.

"Carly?" Jeremiah asked from behind her.

She spun around, finding Zane's older brother standing there frozen in shock, his face drained of color. "Is it real? Is Zane—"

She threw her arms around him, holding on for dear life as she sobbed, "He's alive, Jer. He's been alive this entire time."

Jeremiah's arms encircled her in a fierce hug and the two stood there, just clinging to each other in the very same way they had the day of the terrible tragedy all those years ago.

CHAPTER NINE

"*E*nchantment?" Hope asked. "What exactly does that mean? He's under a spell and can't talk?"

"That seems—" Grace started, but the wind picked up and drowned out what she said next.

Carly wanted to hold onto Jeremiah forever. She hadn't realized exactly how shaken she'd been by her interaction with Zane until she was wrapped in Jeremiah's arms. Her defenses had started to crack, and she was afraid if he let go, she'd completely break apart.

"Let's get you home," Jeremiah whispered in her ear.

"But what about the coven?" She glanced up at him, shaken to her core. She'd wanted to believe that Zane was still alive. Desperately. And she'd been willing to do just about anything to find out the truth. And as happy as she was to have their suspicions confirmed, she also couldn't shake the horror of knowing he'd been alive for more than thirty years and neither of them had known. Worse, it appeared that he was being held against his will. Thirty years of his life wasted. It made Carly want to weep and rage at the same time.

"Can we get together and talk about this later tonight," Grace asked, placing a light hand on Carly's shoulder. "After you've both had time to process?"

Carly untangled herself from Jeremiah, but reached out and grabbed his hand, unable to completely let go.

"That's a good idea," Hope said, moving to stand next to Grace. She studied Carly and then Jeremiah for a moment before adding, "Because if you don't mind me saying so, both of your minds are spinning." She grimaced. "Sorry. It's the mind reading curse. When emotions are strong, there's no controlling it."

"It's all right," Carly said, wondering if the other woman was able to make any sense of all the thoughts running through her head. Because Carly surely couldn't. Her mind was racing.

A phone notification sound went off, and Iris swore under her breath. "Guh. My latest client is texting *again,* demanding that I meet him for a late lunch. Something about needing me to crunch some numbers. I swear, he's the neediest successful business man I've ever met. If he makes me go over my spreadsheets one more time, I think one of us won't make it out alive." She moved to give Carly a one-armed hug. "Should I come by after I'm done? We can brainstorm at your house. Or if you prefer, we can all meet at my place and you can duck out if it gets to be too much." Iris gave her a gentle smile.

"My house," Carly said, desperate to be cocooned in her own space. "Just come when you're done with… What kind of business are you helping him with?"

"He's trying to open a B&B that overlooks the ocean," Iris said. "But there's all kinds of problems with zoning and permits that we have to work through. He decided I was the one to hire since I know all the ins and outs when it comes to regulations in Premonition Pointe."

"*Two* B&Bs," Grace said, her eyes full of glee. "The man just sent me a listing that he wants to look at." She held up her phone, showing a large Victorian in a wooded setting away from the ocean. "He calls it diversification."

Iris pressed her fingertips to her temple and groaned. "Seriously? First of all, two B&Bs in the same town is hardly diversification. And if he starts talking about a second location, the city is going to get cagey about issuing him permits."

Carly tuned them out and turned back to Jeremiah. "I thought you were going to meet me at my house."

He brushed a lock of her windblown blond hair out of her eyes. "I was, but the repair was done faster than they anticipated, and I knew you were here." He shrugged. "I couldn't wait to hear if the finding spell worked."

"It did, and yet, I still have no idea *where* he is," she said, frustrated beyond belief. "In that sense, I failed."

"You found him and now we know he's alive. That's hardly a failure; that's a damned breakthrough." He squeezed her hand and gently tugged her away from the rest of the coven. "Let's go. You clearly need to get off your feet, and I bet you could use some food. How about I take you home and make you something to eat while you—"

"Sit and watch you?" A ripple of anticipation caught her by surprise. Her emotions were all over the place, and yet she still managed to find herself excited by the thought of him cooking in her kitchen. It was just so domestic, so personal. And not at all something she'd have thought possible a few days ago.

"Exactly." He turned, thanked the coven members, and invited them back to Carly's house. Then he wrapped his arm around Carly's shoulder and held her close as they made their way back to their cars.

* * *

"GOAT CHEESE STUFFED manicotti with artichokes? Seriously?" Carly asked from her place at the table. She tapped the end of her pencil on a pad of paper while she watched Jeremiah work. "There is no way you found all those ingredients in my kitchen."

"Did you see me leave or smuggle groceries into this house?" he asked with a smirk.

"I'm sure you managed it somehow," she insisted, certain that she'd never purchased artichokes or manicotti pasta pretty much ever. The goat cheese, however, that was a staple. "Anyone who can throw that meal together and manage to make my house smell like an authentic Italian restaurant must be a magician."

"Just a guy who got tired of take out and decided he'd better learn to cook. You have no idea how many episodes of Emeril Lagasse I watched in order to finally make something edible."

"Edible? My mouth is watering over here. How long until it's done?" she asked.

Jeremiah glanced at the stove clock. "Twenty-five minutes." He poured a couple of glasses of wine and then joined her at the table. After handing her a glass, he peered at her notebook. "Any ideas?"

Carly had been trying to brainstorm what Zane had meant when he'd mouthed the word *enchantment*. So far she'd only written down the obvious. Zane was bound by some sort of enchantment and unable to leave wherever he was being held. "Nothing useful."

He nodded. "That's all I came up with, too. Unless the town he's in is named Enchantment."

"Know any place that's named Enchantment?" Carly asked and took a sip of her wine.

"No." He pulled out his phone and did a quick search. He rattled off some results, "New Mexico is considered the Land of Enchantment, The Enchantments is a place in the Cascades in Washington state, and there's a documentary called *City of Enchantment* that's about big oil and toxic chemicals in the gulf. I suppose any of those could mean something."

Carly groaned. "New Mexico? Washington? The gulf? How does any of that help us? It's not like we can search an entire state or the Washington mountain range. Not easily anyway."

"I will if those are the only leads," Jeremiah said softly.

Carly wrapped her arms around herself, feeling cold even though it was warm in her house from the cooking Jeremiah had done. The idea of him running around after flimsy leads made her stomach ache. If she thought for one minute that any of their ideas had merit, she'd join him. Hell, she'd hire a private investigator or whoever she could find to track him down. Unfortunately, all they really had was a Google search that likely meant nothing. Still, if Jeremiah planned to hop a plane, she'd be right behind him. "I'd go with you."

He studied her and then nodded. "I believe you would."

"I loved—*love*—him, too. Always have. Always will," she said fiercely.

"I know." Jeremiah's eyes misted with unshed tears, but when he blinked, they were gone and all that was left was determination. "And that's why I'm here with you. You're the only other person in this world who misses him as much as I do."

Carly wiped away her own tears and nodded just as she

heard her front door open and the sound of Harlow's voice. She was talking, but not loud enough for Carly to make out her words. "Harlow?" she called. "I'm in the kitchen."

"Did you find some place that delivers Italian? It smells incredible in here," Harlow said as she rounded the corner into the kitchen.

"No one in Premonition Pointe delivers Italian," a familiar woman with short blond curls said with a laugh as she followed Harlow.

"Lex?" Carly said as she stood to greet Grace's niece.

Lex looked taken aback by Carly's approach, but soon enough she found her voice. "Hi, Ms. Preston. It's really, um, wonderful to see you again. And if I didn't tell you before, I just adore all of your movies. I've seen them all hundreds of times."

"Thank you. That's really sweet of you to say. But you must call me Carly," she said. "It's really nice to see you again. And wonderful that you and Harlow have become friends. I hope to see you around more."

Lex's cheeks flushed pink. "Of course. I'd love that, too." She turned to Harlow. "Why didn't you tell me she'd be here? A warning would've helped a lot."

Carly chuckled, embracing the lighthearted emotion. It wasn't often that she encountered someone in Premonition Pointe who cared that much about her acting career. Most of the residents were just used to her by now. Still, it didn't bother her in the least. She liked interacting with fans when they were excited to meet her. It was when they got aggressive and out of hand that she'd always step away and retreat into her hidden sanctuary.

Harlow rolled her eyes. "She's just my Aunt Carly who stands behind a camera for a living. She's a normal person like you and me," she told Lex. "There's nothing to get excited about."

"Well, thanks for that resounding endorsement," Carly said, rolling her eyes. "I think you're special, too."

Harlow grinned at her. "I know. Now, are you gonna share whatever it is you have in the oven, or are you going to force me to drool?"

"There's plenty," Jeremiah said as he rose to deal with the kitchen buzzer that had just gone off.

"Thanks." Harlow grinned and added, "Jeremiah, this is Lex. Lex, Jeremiah."

The two exchanged pleasant hellos before Jeremiah went back to dealing with dinner.

Carly moved to begin setting the table for the four of them. But before she could get the plates out of her cupboard, her phone trilled with a special ringtone. It was a Santana guitar solo, the same one Zane had spent an entire summer learning after his sophomore year in high school.

She knew Jeremiah recognized it because he sucked in a sharp breath and nearly dropped the manicotti.

"It's a nurse from the hospital," she explained. "I didn't want to miss their call." She answered it, and seconds later, she grabbed her keys. "Jeremiah, let's go. John Doe is awake."

CHAPTER TEN

*T*he waiting room in the ICU was busy with almost every seat taken. Carly stood at the nurses' station, waiting to speak to someone as she glanced around and tried to keep her composure. Sadness and worry penetrated her senses, overwhelming her, and she had to blink back tears. Her entire being was weighted down by emotions that didn't belong to her.

Empath. The word echoed in her mind. She'd always been somewhat attuned to others' emotions. Even as a teen she'd often picked up on the feelings of the people she was close to. She'd long speculated that was probably the reason she was so successful at acting. It was relatively easy for her to tap into whatever emotions she needed. But over the last few years, there were a few specific moments when she felt like she was drowning in someone else's pain.

This was one of those moments.

"Carly?" Jeremiah asked, his voice full of concern. "Are you all right?"

She sucked in a breath and nodded. Maybe she was just

drained after the finding spell. "Sorry. I just…" Carly shook her head. "Never mind. It's not important. I guess I'm just anxious to talk to John Doe."

"Ditto. But the nurse did call you. I'm sure we'll get to go in soon," he said, wrapping an arm around her shoulder.

The gesture surprised her but was also starting to feel familiar. It was strange to be comforted by him, but only because it felt so natural. After thirty-plus years, she'd have thought it would've taken her more time to get comfortable with him, but it appeared nothing much had changed for her when it came to Jeremiah. Even after everything that had happened between them, he was still the person who could always manage to make her feel centered. "I hope you're right."

When the nurse finally returned to her station, she met Carly's gaze and frowned.

"What is it?" Carly asked, an ache forming in her gut. "Is John Doe all right? He didn't slip back into a coma, did he?"

The nurse shook her head. "No. Nothing like that. It's just that after I called you, I found out you've been barred from seeing him." Her frown turned into a grimace. "His brother arrived and identified him."

"His brother?" Carly and Jeremiah asked at the same time. Carly clutched his hand. "Who's his brother?"

The nurse shook her head. "I'm not at liberty to divulge any other information. I'm very sorry. But know that Liam—" She clasped her hand over her mouth and shook her head. "I mean John Doe is in good hands now. You no longer need to worry."

"Liam?" Carly asked.

The nurse shook her head quickly and made a hasty retreat.

"Dammit," Carly muttered and turned to Jeremiah. "Brother?"

Jeremiah scanned the room and focused on Phil, the

security guard Carly had tasked with guarding John Doe. "Come on. Let's go ask him what's going on."

"Right." Carly wondered why she hadn't thought of that herself. Jake, her own bodyguard, was standing with the tall, wide-shouldered blond guard over near the windows. They had their heads bent and appeared deep in conversation. She followed Jeremiah across the room.

Both guards turned their attention to them, and before Carly could even start asking him questions, Phil said, "There was a man here who claimed to be John Doe's brother."

Carly nodded. "We know. The nurse told us he was here and that we're barred from seeing him. Did you talk to him?"

Phil nodded. "Casually. I pretended to be here for someone else and tried to strike up a conversation about who he was here visiting. Unfortunately, he didn't really take the bait. He just said his brother and then excused himself to take a call. He was terse with whoever was on the other end and barked that 'he'd take care of it.' After that, he spoke with the nurse and I made sure to eavesdrop a bit. His entire demeanor had changed, and I've got to say, I didn't believe a word he said to her. He flattered her entirely too much and sounded a lot like the slimiest PR guys in Hollywood."

"So you don't believe he's John's brother?" Carly asked.

"He said the man's name is Liam, but no. I don't believe for a minute that he's who he says he is. As soon as he left here, I had someone tail him. He was driving a nondescript white van, and he clearly realized he had a tail right away because he managed to ditch us fairly quickly." His nostrils flared in irritation. "Only someone who is used to evading detection could lose one of our tails so easily."

Carly ground her teeth in frustration. She was certain it wasn't a coincidence that Liam's "brother" was driving a white van, when that's the same type of vehicle that tried to run Jeremiah off the road. Her security had done exactly what she expected of them and more. And still, the man who was likely the key to solving the shooting had gotten away. "Thanks for trying," she said, placing a hand on his arm. "If and when he shows again, will you have more backup? If we knew where that man was staying, it could be the key to everything we're looking for."

"We're on it," Jake said and turned to discuss logistics with Phil.

Jeremiah tugged at Carly's arm, and once they were a few feet from the men, he leaned toward her and said in a hushed tone, "Can't you turn that charm on to get in to see John... or maybe we should call him Liam?"

"I was going to, but the nurse ran away too fast." Carly eyed the nurses' station, wondering if she should try again. But when the nurse she'd spoken to earlier appeared, she took one look at Carly and spun back around, disappearing behind the double doors.

"Looks like she's going to keep avoiding us, too," Jeremiah said, running a frustrated hand though his already-mussed dark hair.

Carly stared at the nurses' station and the double doors behind it, willing the nurse to return. If she had to put on the performance of her life in order to get in and see Liam, that's what she would do.

When it became clear that the original nurse wasn't likely to make another appearance, she straightened her shoulders and strode over to a shorter, blonder nurse who had a sympathetic smile. Carly eyed the nurse's nametag and leaned an elbow on the counter as she flashed the easy smile she'd perfected for photoshoots. "Hey there, Cassie," Carly said easily. "I'm just gonna slip in and say hello to Liam, make sure he has everything he needs." Without waiting for a reply, Carly headed for the double doors as if she owned the place.

"Oh! Ms. Preston, I'm so sorry," the nurse said, sounding nervous and a little bit tongue-tied. "Liam isn't receiving visitors right now."

"What?" Carly turned and gave her what she hoped was an innocent look of surprise. "But his brother was here not too long ago and told me to check in on him before I left for the day."

"Ms. Preston," a woman behind her admonished.

Carly turned to see the first nurse standing and glaring at her in front of the double doors.

"I told you that John Doe wasn't seeing anyone except his brother. I'm going to have to ask you to leave."

Knowing she was beat, Carly nodded once and spun on her heel, frustrated beyond belief that she didn't have any other plan. But one thing she knew for sure; she would not be leaving until she found a way to speak to Liam.

"I take it that didn't go well?" Jeremiah asked when she reached his side.

"Understatement." She grabbed his arm and practically dragged him down the hall away from the waiting area. The last thing they needed was for Nurse Ratched to be watching their every move. Not that she necessarily blamed the other woman. She was just doing her job after all. Still, she wasn't going to let regulations stop her from seeing the man who could lead them right to Zane. "We just need to regroup and figure out how to get past the nurses."

Jeremiah sighed. "Not sure how we're going to do that unless you're planning on doing some sort of invisibility spell."

Carly cocked her head to the side as if contemplating the idea.

"You can do an invisibility spell?" Jeremiah asked.

Laughing, Carly shook her head. "No. But it would come in handy right now."

"That or an invisibility cloak," he said with a wink.

"If only." Carly walked over to the window and stared out over the town of Premonition Pointe. Clouds had rolled in, and it looked like they were in for an evening storm. The weather was mirroring how she felt. There was a storm brewing inside of her, and if they didn't come up with a plan soon, she was likely to barge right through the ICU doors without regard to what anyone said.

"Carly?" a woman said, her voice high-pitched with excitement.

Carly cringed internally. She was in no mood to interact with fans.

"Carly Preston." The woman's voice turned confident and full of affection. "How long has it been? Six, seven years now since we wrapped *All About You*?"

All of the dread that had built up in Carly's chest fled as she realized the fan wasn't a fan at all. She was the best damned matchmaker on the West Coast and had consulted on a film Carly had starred in. They'd become fast friends, even though Carly had to tell her every other day she wasn't interested in a matchmaking service. "Marion Matched," Carly said, shaking her head. "What in the world has brought you to Premonition Pointe? Surely there aren't enough clients in this town for you to expand your matchmaking business all the way up here. Or did you track me down to make good on your threat to finally set me up with my perfect match?"

Marion threw her head back and laughed, making her red

curls bounce around her face. "You do flatter yourself, don't you?" she teased.

"I'm just trying to figure out if I'm going to need to go on the defensive again or if you've conceded that I can find my own date," Carly said with a good-natured shrug.

The other woman eyed Jeremiah for a moment, and her expression changed to one of pure delight. "Looks like you were right." She reached over and gently squeezed Jeremiah's arm. "And who might you be, gorgeous?"

Jeremiah introduced himself and held out his hand.

Marion shook it and grinned at the both of them like a loon. "It's a pleasure. And even more so to learn that Carly finally has a fitting man in her life."

Carly cleared her throat. "Marion, that's not—"

Jeremiah cut her off by asking Marion, "Did Carly date a lot of unsuitable men?"

Marion chuckled. "Yes. Definitely. Men who were too serious, others too ego-driven, but worst of all were the insecure ones. I tell ya, her picker was way off."

"Excuse me," Carly said, placing her hands on her hips. "In my defense, it was Hollywood, and everyone is either neurotic or a selfish bastard. And they're all insecure beyond belief. None of them could handle having their careers overshadowed by mine. It's why I stopped dating men in the film industry."

"Yeah, I know." Marion waved an impatient hand. "But never mind that. Looks like you've gone and finally found your match." She nodded her approval at Jeremiah. "You'll do just fine indeed."

"We're not... I mean, Carly and I are just friends," Jeremiah sputtered. "Old friends. We've known each other since we were teenagers."

"Uh-huh." Marion's grin widened. "Even better. It's good

for her to be challenged by someone who doesn't see her as *the Carly Preston*. She needs someone who sees her outside of that world. An equal. Someone who respects her not because of her movies or her bank account, but because of the person she's become."

Jeremiah glanced at Carly but quickly looked away as if it was too hard to look at her. "Uh, well, I guess I will always think of her as Zane's best friend instead of some elusive movie star who hangs out at fancy parties and flies off to Rome at a moment's notice."

"I've never once flown off anywhere on a moment's notice," Carly said rolling her eyes. "Everyone knows I'm a planner when it comes to travel."

"Did you know that?" Marion asked Jeremiah.

"Yes," he said firmly. "Even when we were kids, Carly always planned everything ahead. She's not great with spontaneity."

"Hey, I resent that. Who doesn't love a little spontaneity? I can be flexible… just not when it comes to flying out of the country. There's nothing wrong with being prepared," Carly insisted.

"Absolutely," he said with a teasing grin. "Remember that time we decided to take an impromptu trip up the coast? You wouldn't let us leave until you not only got hotel reservations for all four nights in different towns but also planned out our dinners. I mean, back then, I'm sure it was completely normal to have an entire book of restaurants to choose from."

Carly snorted with laughter. "It wasn't a book. It was a magazine. And fine. Maybe spontaneity isn't my thing. But when it comes to exploring new places, no one is better than me at finding the best spots."

"I won't argue with that," he said.

Marion cleared her throat. "Well, that was fun to watch."

"What was?" they both asked in unison.

"That bit of mating-ritual theater. If you two don't end up together, it will be a tragedy. I've never met two people so perfect for each other."

"Marion," Carly warned. "Stop. It's not like that."

"Not yet." She grinned at both of them. "But there's time." She glanced at her watch and grimaced. "Speaking of time, I need to get going. My aunt is waiting for me. Poor thing had heart surgery two days ago and while she's doing just fine, she hates being here. Hospitals aren't her thing. So I'm spending as much time with her as possible to keep her entertained." She paused and eyed Carly. "Who are you here for? It's not Harlow, is it?"

"Oh, no. Harlow is doing great. We're here for... uh..." Carly looked at Jeremiah helplessly. She trusted Marion, but she wasn't sure Jeremiah would want her to broadcast that they thought Zane might be alive.

"A man was shot in front of Carly's house," Jeremiah explained. "We've been waiting for him to wake up so we can find out what happened that night. Unfortunately, someone who is claiming to be his brother was here and has barred us from seeing him. But I've met him briefly before, and I'm pretty sure he doesn't have a brother, so now we think he's still in danger. We're trying to figure out a way to get in to see him before the shooter finishes the job."

Carly nodded when Marion glanced at her. "Yeah. That just about covers it. As you can imagine, I'm pretty upset about this. That poor man. After seeing him nearly bleeding out in the middle of my street, I just feel... connected to him somehow."

"Of course, you do," Marion said sympathetically. "You've

always been a bit of an empath. It's not surprising that you've formed a bond with him after all that trauma."

"What?" Carly asked as if she hadn't just clearly heard what Marion had said.

Marion frowned. "Didn't you realize that empaths form connections when emotions are high? You'll likely forever be linked now."

Carly shook her head. "No... I mean, yes. I knew that. I just didn't realize you knew I had empath abilities."

"I think they're stronger now than they used to be," Marion mused. "But I'm pretty sure you always had that gift." She slipped her arm through Carly's and added, "Now come on. You're going in to see my aunt. And if you happen to need to excuse yourself to use the restroom or something, it's no problem. I'll wait until you're done before leaving so we'll be seen walking in and out together. The nurses never need to know if you get turned around and end up in another patient's room, now do they?"

"Marion," Carly said, clutching her arm. "You're brilliant. Thank you. You have no idea how much we appreciate this."

"Oh, I think I have an idea." She turned her head and gave Jeremiah a knowing smile before she said, "Do me a favor and don't let this one get away, will you? She deserves the kind of love you have brewing inside of you."

Before Jeremiah could answer, Marion whisked Carly away and through the doors to the ICU.

CHAPTER ELEVEN

"Hey! You're not supposed to be back here," Nurse Ratched called as she ran down the hallway toward Carly.

"Francine?" Marion said with a manufactured air of confusion. "Is there a problem? I was told visiting hours didn't end until seven."

"Yes, there is a problem," Francine said, placing her hands on her hips and glaring at Carly. "I already told Ms. Preston that John Doe isn't taking visitors. She can't be here."

"John Doe?" Marion glanced at Carly and then back to Francine. "Carly's here to see my aunt. I ran into her in the waiting room, and because my aunt is such a huge fan, I practically begged her to come along with me. And even though she protested and said she had places to be this afternoon, I finally convinced her by bribing her with my famous coffee cake. There was no debate after that. Carly's a sucker for my coffee cake. Always has been. Right, Car?"

Carly took a step closer to Marion, deciding that her friend deserved that best actress award sitting on her mantle at home more than Carly did. Because the show Marion was putting on was nothing short of brilliant. "Right. I'm just here to cheer up Marion's aunt."

Francine's face turned a bright shade of red as her fists clenched. But then she blew out a breath and seemed to force herself to calm down. "All right, but if you visit anyone besides Ms. Matched, I'll be forced to call security."

Carly saluted her and had to hold back a smirk as the nurse spun around and rushed off to another room.

"She really doesn't seem to like you much," Marion said with a chuckle.

"She did until about a half hour ago," Carly said with a sigh. "I wonder if she's going to perch right outside Liam's room just to make sure I don't step out of line."

"Okay, John Doe is Liam, right? I'm not confused about that?"

"Yes." Carly waved her forward. "Nurse Ratched—er, Francine—accidentally used his first name in front of me. So while she's still calling him John around me, I know his real name."

Marion eyed her for a moment. "You do seem to know how to get into trouble, don't you?"

"Me?" Carly asked, genuinely surprised. "No. I'm actually fairly boring. This is just—"

"Please. You solved the mystery of what happened to Harlow and helped save her. Your life is not boring."

"That was…" Carly shrugged. "She's my niece. I'd do anything for her."

"Of course, you would." Marion tugged her down another hallway. "Never mind. Let's make this look good so you can go find Liam and do what you need to do." She stopped in front of a door and said, "I wasn't kidding when I said my auntie is a huge fan. In fact, I should warn her first before you just pop in."

"Okay," Carly said, amused. "What's her name?"

"Lucy. Just give me a few seconds." Marion disappeared through the door.

A few seconds later, a high-pitched squeal came from inside the room. Carly took it to mean that Marion had shared the news. She pushed the door open and poked her head in. "Lucy? Is it okay if I come in and say hi?"

The older woman had the back of her hand pressed to her forehead as if she were ready to faint. Only there weren't any signs of that happening. No. Instead, her cheeks were flushed red and her eyes were dancing with delight. "Yes, my dear. Come in. Please. I can't believe Marion made you wait outside. You must come sit by me and tell me absolutely everything you know about that hunky Ray Rochester. I hear he's the best kisser in Hollywood. Well, and good at other things too, but I don't want to presume you'd know about that."

Carly couldn't help giggling with Aunt Lucy. Her personality was far to infectious. Carly was happy to dish about her costar from a movie twenty years earlier, who'd turned out to actually be a terrible kisser and an even worse date. However, Carly kept that to herself and let the older woman have her fantasies.

Marion stood back, watching with a grin on her face.

"What?" Carly asked her when she met her eye.

"Nothing." Marion shook her head. "Just enjoying that sparkle in Aunt Lucy's eyes."

"I always have a sparkle in my eyes," Lucy huffed.

"I know. It's just a little brighter today." Marion moved to stand next to the bed and took Lucy's hand in hers. "I'm glad you seem to be feeling better."

"Well, I couldn't exactly act the curmudgeon with Carly Preston here, could I?" Lucy patted her hair as if just now realizing she might have bedhead.

"That was my plan." Marion gave Carly a grateful smile. Then her tone turned teasing as she added, "Now give me and Lucy a minute. I need to scold her about torturing her nurses."

"Don't scold her too much. I think Nurse Ratched might deserve it." Carly gave Lucy a thumbs up before she slipped out of the room. As soon as she found herself back in the hall, her heartrate sped up and her nerves started to take over. She had no doubt that Francine would be true to her word and call security if she found Carly in Liam's room. And if the press got wind of that, it'd be one hell of a shitshow. Carly had to risk it, though. She just had to.

Striding down the hall, she spied the bathrooms off to her right but ignored them as she kept walking. There were charts outside of each room with last names stamped on the folders. Was Liam's stamped with Doe or something else? Carly stifled a groan and continued to search.

Voices sounded behind her, making her want to duck into the nearest room. But her cover was that she was looking for the restroom if anyone asked. They didn't. In fact, the doctor who passed her was talking to a colleague when he said, "Doe's gunshot wound is healing nicely, but we still need to keep him a few days. His memory loss is concerning, considering he doesn't have any obvious brain injury. It's almost as if it's psychological."

Carly froze. They were talking about Liam. John Doe. Which room had they come from? She really had no idea. They'd just appeared behind her. She turned around and asked, "Excuse me?"

The doctor blinked at her as if he'd just noticed she was in the hallway. "Yes?"

"Can you tell me where Liam's room is?" She held her breath, hoping she wasn't making a huge mistake.

"Liam?" the doctor looked at his colleague. "Any idea who she's talking about?"

He shook his head.

"The patient with the gunshot wound. He's my cousin. You know him as John Doe."

"Doe. Yes. He's in 2D. Lucky man. If that bullet had been any farther to the right, he might have bled out."

Carly winced. "Well, thank the goddess for bad aim, right?"

"Right." The doctor's pager went off. "Time to go. They need us in surgery." Without taking another look at Carly, they rushed off.

Relieved they were gone, Carly hurried over to room 2D. After peeking in and finding Liam alone, she hurried inside and closed the door behind her.

Liam's tired gaze landed on her, and he frowned. "Are you another nurse?"

Carly let out a nervous laugh. "No. You don't remember me?"

He squinted and studied her as if trying to place her. "You look sort of familiar, but no. You're not my mother or something, are you?"

That made her laugh out loud. "No. Definitely not. Do you remember why you're in the hospital?"

He shook his head. "No. But they told me it's because I was shot outside some actress's house." His brows pinched together. "Why would I have been outside an actress's house?"

Carly moved over to the side of the bed. Liam's skin was very pale, and he appeared even thinner than before. But his eyes were alert even if they were skeptical. "I'm that actress. Carly Preston. Does that name ring a bell?"

"No." He stared up at her and then shook his head again. "No idea who you might be. Do we know each other?"

"We don't. Or at least we didn't until that night."

"Is that why you're here now? Out of some sort of moral obligation to make sure I don't die?" Skepticism and distrust rolled off him. And why shouldn't it? Carly had a feeling that whatever life he'd led over the years had trained him to not trust anyone.

"No moral obligation. A personal one." She pulled out the picture that he'd given to Jeremiah. The one with the four of them in the photobooth. "Do you recognize this?"

His eyes widened, and he whispered, "Lazer."

Carly's heart nearly exploded in her chest. Even if he didn't remember anything else, he knew Zane. "His real name is Zane. Did you know that?"

"Zane?" He said it as if he were feeling it out. Then he said, "No. Lazer."

"Do you remember asking Jeremiah for help to find him?"

Liam narrowed his eyes at her. "Who's Jeremiah?"

She tapped his image in the photo. "Zane's brother."

He didn't say anything at first as his face was scrunched in concentration. Then he blew out a breath. "I don't know. Everything is fuzzy. Like I'm waking up from a crazy, disjointed dream."

"I understand." Carly glanced at the door, wondering exactly how much time she had. Probably not much. So she pressed on, needing to get as much information out of him as possible. "Do you have a brother?"

"Not that I know of. Why?" He started to raise his bed so that he was in a sitting position. The movement made him wince, but he didn't let the pain stop him. By the time he was sitting fully upright, he was panting and looked flushed as if he'd just worked out.

"A man came to the hospital and claimed to be your brother. He says your name is Liam."

"No, I'm not Hun—" His eyes widened, and his breath caught as he added, "That's what Lazer called me." Tears shone in his dark eyes as he was overcome with emotion.

"Oh, honey." Carly instinctively took his hand in hers. "I know. I love Zane—I mean Lazer, too. We were best friends for a very long time. The reason I'm here is that Jeremiah and I want desperately to help you find him."

Liam's eyes snapped to hers. "Are you serious?"

"Very serious. We thought he died in an accident many years ago, or we'd have been looking for him this entire time." She sat down on the edge of the bed. "If there's anything you can remember about where he is, that would be really helpful."

He pulled his hand from her grip and turned to stare at the wall. When he turned back, he just shook his head. "I don't remember anything. I didn't even remember him until you showed me this picture." He ran a finger over Zane's face.

"It's all right. I'm sure we can work on it." She paused because there was something she needed to say but didn't know how, considering they'd just met and she barely knew him. "I think you're still in danger. The man who claims to be your brother... Well, I think he might work for the people who shot you."

Liam nodded once and then let his head fall back against the pillow. Then he threw his covers off and swung his legs over the side of the bed. "Looks like it's time to leave then."

"What?" Carly asked, putting a hand out to stop him. "You can't leave yet. You just had surgery. You need—"

"I need to be someplace where this man who calls himself my brother can't get to me. Do you think this is that place?"

Carly shook her head. Hell, she'd managed to get herself in with very little effort.

"Right. Bullet wound or not, I need to ditch this hell hole." He nearly doubled over when he pushed himself off the bed.

"Hold on. I've got you!" Carly called as she rushed around to help him.

"Thanks," he said, through his shortened breath. "Any idea of where my clothes might be?"

"Clothes?" Carly asked stupidly. Then she recovered. "I doubt there's anything left of them. Everything was covered in blood from that night, and the EMTs probably cut them off of you."

"Right." He pushed a hand through his dark, shaggy hair. "Well, it's going to be awkward leaving in this hospital gown, but there seems to be no choice."

Carly was about to offer to run out and pick some things up for him, but the door swung open, and Nurse Ratched stormed in.

"Carly Preston!" She wagged her index finger in Carly's direction as she picked up the phone receiver on the wall. "I told you I'd have to call security if you came into Liam's room."

"I want her here," Liam insisted. "Don't you know movie stars cheer up the infirm?"

Carly raised an eyebrow at him. He sure was quick-witted for someone who could barely remember details of his own life.

He shrugged. "It's true." Then he turned his attention back to the nurse. "Besides, it doesn't matter. I'm leaving anyway."

"You can't leave!" she cried, her eyes wide with disbelief. "You're still on an IV for the goddess's sake."

He reached over and pulled the needle out of his wrist. "Not anymore. Now I'm just a broke son of a bitch who's leaving the hospital against medical advice."

"But—" She stared again. "Where will you go?"

He shrugged. "I'll find somewhere. I always do."

Carly felt the lie as it passed his lips. This man had nowhere to go, but staying in the hospital could be potentially deadly. "He's staying with me," Carly blurted before she could talk herself out of it. Hell, she barely knew this man. He could be any sort of criminal. He could sell information about her to the press, or he could be lying about everything just to scam her out of money.

It was stupid to bring him into her home, not without having Jake vet him with a background check at the very least. But on the other hand, he'd be safer there than anywhere else. And if they were going to find Zane, they needed Liam alive. Not to mention, she had no desire to see the man hurt again.

"I am?" Liam asked with his eyebrows at the top of his forehead.

"Yes. We talked about it before Nurse Ra—I mean, Nurse Francine came in. Remember?"

He shook his head.

"That's because you have that memory problem." Carly smiled sweetly at him. "Now put those slippers on, and let's go. The sooner we get you home, the sooner you can have some real clothes."

Nurse Ratched narrowed her eyes at them both. "What exactly is going on here? I don't think either of you should go anywhere until—"

The door banged open, and everyone froze when the man who claimed to be Liam's brother brandished a gun and pointed it right at him.

CHAPTER TWELVE

"*C*harles! What in the hell do you think you're doing?" Nurse Ratched cried as she jumped in front of Liam's bed, blocking the man who claimed to be Liam's brother from shooting him.

"You'll want to get out of the way, Francine," Charles said, his expression so cold that it actually made Carly shiver.

"Not on your life," she hissed at him.

Carly had a newfound respect for Nurse Ratched. The way she was willing to sacrifice herself for her patient was downright heroic.

He shrugged. "Fine. I can't leave any witnesses anyway."

Francine's eyes widened with horror as she reached for the call button on the side of Liam's bed.

"I've already told the authorities everything," Liam said, twisting to look over the nurse's shoulder. "You won't get far before they haul you in for every crime you've ever committed."

Liam's statement was so vague that Carly knew Charles must be aware that he was bluffing. But still, the man faltered just long enough to give Carly an opening. She desperately wished she'd taken that martial arts class that had been advertised at her gym for the last six months, but at least she had basic self-defense experience. It was enough to give her the confidence to not hesitate to strike the vile man. She kicked out, taking him off guard and sweeping his legs out from underneath him. He went down with a roar of rage.

Carly pounced, jumping on top of him and grabbing his wrist, trying to force him to drop the gun. Her heart was pounding as her adrenaline spurred her on.

"You bitch," he spat and bucked up, easily throwing her off him.

Her only saving grace was that she never let go of his wrist, and as she jerked off him, she slammed his wrist into the hard floor.

He grunted and reached for her, catching her by the back of her hair. He yanked hard, making her eyes sting with tears. Pain radiated from every inch of her scalp, but no way was she giving up.

"Let go," he growled.

"Drop it," she countered, staring into his pale ice-blue eyes. There was no feeling there, no emotion. Just determination. She knew that he would not stop until they were all dead.

His grip tightened on her hair, and Carly wondered if he was going to rip it out by the roots. "You're going to regret—" His eyes widened as he froze and then suddenly his entire body went slack.

Carly freed herself from his grip and looked up to find Nurse Ratched with one hand on her heart and the other holding a needle.

With shaking hands, Francine put the needle down on a tray and then sank to her knees.

"Damn. That was badass," Liam said from his spot at the side of his bed. He'd managed to get to his feet, but he was clutching the edge of the bed to keep from faltering.

"Thank you, Francine," Carly said, letting out a long breath. "You saved us."

"No. I think you did," she said, holding out a hand to help Carly to her feet. "If you hadn't attacked him, there's no way I would've had time to prepare that needle. And surely he'd have kept his word and killed us all." She sucked in a deep breath and added, "I'm sorry about the way I treated you. I really thought I was doing what was best for the patient."

"I understand," Carly said. "I really do. Let's just be glad we're all walking away from this."

The nurse nodded, and before she could say another word, the door crashed open and a doctor and a male nurse rushed in.

The tall, lanky doctor stopped in his tracks and stared at the man on the floor, then his dark eyes fixated on the gun. He turned to the nurse right behind him. "Get security. Now."

The male nurse nodded and hurried out of the room.

The doctor kneeled next to Charles and pressed his fingertips to the pulse point on his neck. "Get a blood pressure reading," he ordered Francine.

Carly noted that Nurse Ratched was grinding her teeth as she did as she was told.

"He had a gun and threatened to shoot all of us," she told the doctor.

"What did you give him?" the doctor asked.

Francine rattled off the name of some medication that Carly had never heard of, and once she had his blood pressure, she barked the number to the doctor and got back to her feet. "I'm done here."

"The police will want a statement," he said.

"Fine. I'll wait in the break room." She glanced over at Carly and Liam. "Be safe."

Carly nodded at her and then guided Liam back to the bed.

"I'm not staying here," Liam insisted.

"I know. But we do need to make a statement to the police," Carly said. "You're not going to last long on your feet."

He grumbled but did as he was told. Carly sat right next to him, and they both watched as orderlies put Charles on a rolling gurney while the hospital security handcuffed him to the rails. Charles moaned as if he was regaining consciousness. Carly got up to move to his side. When his eyes fluttered open, she stared down at him and said, "I'm making it my mission to ensure they lock you up and throw away the key."

He licked at his dry lips and croaked out in a barely audible voice, "If you do that, you'll never see Zane again."

"Zane?" she repeated, her body nearly vibrating with the need to shake Charles. "Where is he?" she insisted.

But Charles closed his eyes and went limp as he passed out again.

"Wake up!" she cried. "I need you to tell me where Zane is!"

"Ma'am, you're going to have to step away from the patient," the doctor said.

"He's not the patient," Carly insisted. "Liam is. This piece of trash is a criminal."

"In this case, the criminal is also a patient," the doctor said in the calmest voice Carly had ever heard.

Rationally, Carly knew the man was only doing his job, but that didn't stop her from wanting to scream at him. Charles had been ready to kill them all. He didn't deserve the doctor's help. If it hadn't been for Francine, there was a very good chance that she'd have never made it out of the hospital, and that realization was more than a little overwhelming. Her body had started to shake, and her insides were clenched with nerves.

"Carly," Liam said softly. "Come over here." He patted the side of his bed, indicating that she should sit next to him.

She went willingly, and when he took her hand in his, she squeezed, grateful for the human contact. "As soon as we make our statements, I'm getting you out of here," she whispered to him. "After this incident, it's clear it's not safe for you here."

"Okay," he said, sounding exhausted.

The doctor looked up from where he was leaning over Charles and narrowed his eyes at them. "Mr. Jones isn't ready to be discharged."

Carly raised her eyebrows. "Mr. Jones?" Then she looked at Liam. "Is that your last name?"

Liam closed his eyes and shook his head slightly. "I have no idea."

"That's what it says on his chart," the doctor said, sounding impatient. "Regardless, I strongly suggest that the patient stay here for at least twenty-four more hours. He needs observation, and we need to finish out his intravenous antibiotic."

Carly met Liam's gaze. "I don't like it. But if you want to stay, I can have security stationed right outside your door. Or if you come home with me, I can hire a private nurse to care for you."

"Who are you, my fairy godmother?" he asked, shaking his head. "It must be nice to be richer than God."

"I'm not richer than— You know what? It doesn't matter. What's the point of having money if I can't use it for good?" she asked.

"Sure. Okay. I'll come with you," he said as his eyes drifted closed. "Anywhere is better than here."

Not long after that, Liam drifted off to sleep, and Carly waited by his side until the police had come to take their statements.

"I'll go find you some clothes to wear, then we can go," Carly said to Liam once the police left the room. "Hold tight, okay?"

He nodded and turned to stare out the window.

Carly squeezed his hand once more and hurried out of the room. She spotted her security guard, Jake, first and made a beeline for him. After speaking with him for a few moments, he took off to secure some clothes for her new houseguest, and Carly headed over to Jeremiah where he was sitting with Marion.

They were facing away from her in plastic chairs, and Marion had her hand on Jeremiah's arm as she said, "One day soon, you're going to be ready to move forward. Just be open to it, and you'll know when the time is right."

"Ready to move forward on what?" Carly asked, her heart pounding wildly against her ribcage. Marion was a very successful matchmaker. Was she seriously priming him for some sort of love match? Jealousy flared to life in Carly's chest, and she wanted to demand that Marion stay far away from him. Now wasn't the time for that nonsense. They were busy trying to find Zane.

But the truth whispered in the back of her mind that timing wasn't the issue. It was the fact that even after all the years that had passed, Carly was still picturing herself by Jeremiah's side. And the idea of him with anyone else was unthinkable.

"You know... life, love, the pursuit of happiness." Marion winked at Carly, stood, and handed Jeremiah her card. "Call me if you need… anything." Then she grabbed Carly into a fierce hug. "We heard about the commotion, but no one would let us in to see how you were. I'm glad you're okay."

Carly hugged her back and felt her angst over Jeremiah melt away. After what she'd been through, she was just grateful to be safe and sound. "Thanks."

Marion pulled away and held her at arm's length as she added, "I'll be in town for a while to look after my aunt. When things calm down, we have to get together for lunch. Promise?"

"Promise," Carly said with a nod.

As soon as the other woman walked away, Jeremiah swept Carly into his own fierce hug. "Dammit, Carly. Don't do that to me again. I almost came unglued waiting to find out if you were all right."

She clung to him, pressing her cheek against his chest. His heart was thundering in her ear. Clearly, he'd heard about the gunman. "I'm sorry. I should have let you know we were both fine. But then we had to wait to make statements, and well, we were both shaken up."

His arms tightened around her, and he murmured, "No need to apologize. It was just really hard not knowing if you were okay. I don't think I'd survive it if I lost you, too." His voice broke on the word *you*, making Carly cling to him tighter.

"I'm not going anywhere," she choked out, overcome with emotion. Carly pulled back and stared up at him, seeing the same anguish she felt coming off him as well. She swallowed hard. "I promise."

"No one can make that promise, Carly. We both know that," he said, tucking a lock of hair behind her ear. "Just promise you'll be careful."

Carly wanted to ask him *why now*. After all the years that

had passed, why did he care so much *now*? But she knew the answer. All the trauma from thirty-plus years ago had flooded back. He could no longer put everything aside and pretend that she didn't exist. That ended when he realized he needed her help to find his brother. She just didn't know if all the emotion he was feeling was genuinely directed at her or if it was just a manifestation of needing someone to lean on while they tried to find Zane.

"Carly," he said more urgently. "Promise me."

"I promise," she said quietly, and let him pull her into his arms once more.

CHAPTER THIRTEEN

"Are you sure this is a good idea?" Jeremiah asked Carly as they watched Jake and Phil help Liam into her house.

"No," she said honestly. Neither of them knew Liam. She was fully aware that he could be a complete fraud and out to scam her. But something in her gut told her she needed to trust him. That he really did believe that Zane was alive, and he wanted to find him. It wasn't something she could ignore, and she was willing to do what it took to keep him safe. "I don't think there's any other choice though. Besides, Phil and Jake are here."

"Yeah, outside," he muttered, but he didn't push the conversation further.

Carly followed the men into her house, and after Liam was settled into a downstairs guest room, she made her way back out into the living room where she found Harlow and Lex cuddled under a blanket together. They were watching a rom-com about a gay couple coming to terms with moving from New York City to a small town in Tennessee.

"Hey," Carly said, smiling at them. She loved that her niece and Lex had gotten closer. Harlow deserved good friendships. "What's going on?"

"Nothing." Harlow scooted away from Lex, leaving her with the blanket, and wrapped her arms around her knees in a defensive position. "Just watching a movie."

Carly eyed her, suddenly suspicious. Why had she scrambled away from Lex so quickly as if she were doing something wrong?

"Stop looking at me like that," Harlow insisted. "There's nothing wrong with watching a gay Hallmark movie."

"Of course, there isn't," Carly said, blinking at her in surprise. "You know I love Hallmark movies. Why would there be anything wrong with it?"

"There's not." Harlow got up and started walking toward the kitchen. "Lex? You want anything? I'm grabbing a cupcake."

"Another one?" Lex asked in surprise. "I swear, we've eaten everything that isn't nailed down already."

"Oh come on. What's the point of a sleepover unless we gorge ourselves on sugar?" Harlow said.

Lex laughed but waved her off. "I'm fine with my water."

"Your loss." Harlow hurried into the kitchen, leaving Carly wondering what had just happened. She turned to Jeremiah, who was standing behind her. "I'll be right back. I need to talk to Harlow for a second."

"Sure." He glanced at the hallway. "I'm going to go talk to Liam and see if I can jog his memory a little."

Carly had the insane desire to press up onto her tiptoes and kiss him on the cheek, but she refrained. The moment they'd shared at the hospital had passed. There was no point in making things weird. She gave him a tired smile. "Good luck."

He paused as his brow furrowed. "Are you okay? After what happened at the hospital, anyone would be shaken up. Do you need anything? Is there anything I can do?"

This time she couldn't resist, and Carly pressed a kiss to his cheek. "Thank you. I appreciate the concern, but I'm okay at the moment. I'll probably crash soon, but first, I'm going to go talk to Harlow for a minute. I need to let her know what happened before she hears about it from someone else."

He nodded and then leaned down and kissed the top of her head. "Okay. I'm here if you need me."

Guh. The man was being far too kind, and she just knew that she was setting herself up to get her heart broken, but she couldn't stop herself from falling for him all over again. "Thanks," she said thickly as she watched him disappear down the hall toward the guest room.

"You like him," Lex said from her place on the couch. "A lot."

Carly turned her attention to Grace's niece. "It's that obvious?" Of course it was. She was probably walking around with moon eyes after their interaction at the hospital.

"The only way you could be more obvious is if you had a flashing neon sign over your head." Lex grinned at her. "It reminds me of how I was right before I got together with Bronwyn. Grace took a picture of me and honestly, Carly, the look on my face in that photo is downright embarrassing. Bronwyn still gives me shit for it."

"So you're saying I look like a fool?" Carly asked as her lips twitched in amusement.

"Yep, but you manage to still look radiant, so it's a better look for you than me." She chuckled and then turned, eyeing the kitchen. "Do you think Harlow got lost in there?"

Carly shrugged. "I was just going to go chat with her for a minute anyway." She waved at Lex and strode into her kitchen where she found Harlow sitting at the bar with her head in her hands. "Hey, what's wrong?" she asked and placed a light hand on her shoulder.

Harlow jerked her head up and blinked away tears. "Nothing."

"It doesn't look like nothing." Carly sat down next to her and took one of her niece's hands in both of hers. "You know you can tell me anything, right? Even if it's about you and Lex. No judgement here."

"Me and Lex? What are you talking about?" Harlow jerked back, looking offended.

Carly winced. Had she read everything wrong? She'd walked in on them cuddling, and when Harlow noticed Carly, she'd rushed to put distance between them. And now she was sitting in the kitchen with her head in her hands as if she was stressed about something. Carly assumed that might be because Lex lived with her girlfriend Bronwyn, and if Harlow was developing feelings for her, it made sense that she'd be upset. "Sorry. I may have jumped to the wrong conclusion."

"I'd say so." Harlow stood and crossed her arms over her chest. "And I never said I like women… like that, did I?"

"No." Carly studied her niece in confusion. The pair of them had always been close and never had trouble communicating with each other. Carly told her niece everything. She was her best friend. But the woman standing in front of her was closed off and defensive, and she wasn't acting herself at all. "I didn't mean to offend you, Harlow. I only wanted to make sure you knew that if there's anything you want to talk about, I'm here. Always."

Harlow closed her eyes and after a moment, she nodded. "I know. There's nothing going on with me and Lex. We're just friends."

"But there is *something* going on," Carly hedged. "Right?"

"Yeah." She blew out a breath. "I'm just not ready to talk about it."

Carly squeezed her hand. "Okay. You don't have to; you know that. I'm here when you need me."

Harlow tugged her aunt closer and gave her a hug. "I love you. I'm sorry I'm in this mood. It's not you."

"No need to apologize." Carly held her niece for a long moment before she took a deep breath and said, "You might not be ready to talk, but there's something I need to tell you."

They both sat back down on the stools, and Carly told her all about the incident at the hospital. When she was finally done, Harlow gaped at her.

"You seriously took down a gunman at the hospital? And then you brought some stranger home to stay with us?" She widened her eyes and in a shocked tone, asked, "Who *are* you, Wonder Woman?"

Carly let out a bark of laughter. "I don't think I'd look good in her red and blue bodysuit. I'd need to lose about twenty pounds before I stuffed this old body into anything that formfitting."

"Please. You're gorgeous," Harlow said, rolling her eyes. "If you don't believe me, ask Mr. Handsome who keeps looking at you like he's a wolf who hasn't eaten in weeks."

"He does not," Carly insisted.

"Yes, he does. Just not when you're watching." She smirked. "You don't have to take my word for it. Let's just see where he ends up sleeping tonight."

Carly rolled her eyes. "In a guest room, where he belongs."

"Sure, Auntie. We'll see." Harlow reached over and grabbed a cupcake then waved as she left the kitchen to return to Lex and their sleepover party.

After making a special cup of herbal tea for Liam, Carly went to find her newest houseguest. She found him propped up in bed, staring out at the moonlight glistening off the ocean. His jaw was clenched, and his shoulders were hunched with tension.

"What's going on in here?" she asked tentatively as she put the tea on a nightstand and waved at it. "It's an herbal tea. It should help you heal."

Jeremiah stood with his arms crossed over his chest, glaring at Liam. "He knows something he's not telling us."

Carly switched her gaze from Jeremiah to Liam and back again. "Explain."

"He knows things about Zane, like his birthmark on his neck and that jagged scar on his foot. And the sound of his laugh." Jeremiah's voice was strangled with emotion. "But he won't tell me how he knows him or where he last saw him. He's holding back."

Pure frustration emoted from Liam, making Carly's skin itch. She glanced at him again and could see the struggle in his eyes. "Is that true?" Carly asked him, trying to keep any hint of accusation from her tone.

"No," Liam practically growled. "I already told your boyfriend that I don't know where he is, or where we were, or why. I just know that I need to find him, and I don't have anyone else to turn to. At least, I don't think I do."

Carly put her hand on Jeremiah's arm and leaned into him as she said, "I don't think he's lying. There's no deception coming from him."

"How do you know that?" Jeremiah asked, his muscles flexing with just as much tension as Liam's. "Haven't you considered that he might just be a really good actor?"

A laugh bubbled up from the back of her throat. "Jeremiah. Consider who you're talking to," she said in a teasing tone. "Don't you think I can recognize acting when I see it?"

He blinked down at her, his jaw clenched. But then his face relaxed as he blew out a breath. "Right. Okay. But none of this makes any sense. He can't even tell me where he's from or if he has any family."

Carly went to sit next to Liam. They hadn't talked much while they were waiting for the police to come take their statements at the hospital. They'd both been in a state of shock. Besides, she hadn't wanted to get his story while a bunch of people were milling around. "Can you start from the beginning? How did you end up looking for Jeremiah?"

Liam visibly swallowed and let out a deep sigh. "I keep asking myself that, and I'm just not sure. It's like my memory is scrambled or something."

"An effect from the shooting, maybe?" she asked.

He shrugged one shoulder. "How would I know? The only thing I remember clearly is Lazer giving me a photo and telling me to find those people. That they'd help me. You two are those people."

Carly and Jeremiah shared a long look. His statement was so vague and gave them nothing at all to help them find Zane. If it was even true that he was still alive. But Liam had the photobooth picture from that day, and it was largely still intact, though slightly curled from what looked like water damage.

Carly asked, "Can you describe the surroundings of that

day when he gave you the photo? What do you remember besides what he told you?"

His eyes flashed with pure anguish for just a moment. Then he opened his mouth to speak before closing it and shaking his head. "I don't know."

Carly didn't believe that for a second. The rush of emotion that was swirling in the room was enough that it was starting to make her tear up. "You're going to need to be honest with us if we're going to work together to find Zane. We can't help if you're holding back vital information."

"I'm not holding anything back," he said coolly and went back to staring out the window.

"Did you know that Carly is an empath?" Jeremiah asked from his spot across the room.

"What?" Both Carly and Liam said at the same time. It was true that she was an empath, but it wasn't something that Carly advertised or even necessarily realized when they were younger. And it certainly wasn't something that they'd ever talked about before.

Jeremiah gave her an exasperated look. "You've always been in tune with other people's emotions. You're even more so now. Don't think I haven't noticed." He turned his attention to Liam. "She has an uncanny sense of always knowing how other people are feeling. I'd bet that means she can tell when someone is being truthful, too."

Liam cut his gaze to Carly. "Is he right? Are you like some mystical lie detector or something?"

The way he said it made her chuckle. "I wouldn't put it that way, but I'm usually able to tell when people aren't being completely honest. It's the guilt and inner turmoil that gives them away."

"Dammit," he muttered and ran a hand through his

shaggy sandy-blond hair. There were small worry lines around his eyes, and for the first time she tried to guess his age. Early forties maybe? It was hard to tell with the healing scrapes on one side of his face. Finally, he looked Carly straight in the eyes and said, "It's just that I don't know what's true and what isn't. I don't trust my memories."

There was no denying that his statement was one hundred percent true. She could feel heartfelt emotion behind his words. She gave him a sympathetic smile and said, "I believe you."

Liam's eyes misted over before he covered them with his hand and said, "Thank you."

Carly wanted to wrap him up in her arms and comfort him. The immense relief he was experiencing was slightly overwhelming even for her. Instead of smothering him, she reached for the tea on the nightstand and handed it to him. "Drink this and then we'll let you get some rest. We can talk more in the morning."

He nodded and then did as she asked and drained the tea.

Carly could feel the disapproval wafting off Jeremiah. She understood his frustration. He was desperate to find his brother. But there really wasn't anything they could do that night, and they'd be better at forming a plan in the morning once they got some rest. She took the cup from Liam, told him where he could find extra toiletries, and then tugged Jeremiah out of the room.

"Tomorrow?" Jeremiah asked as soon as they were in the hallway.

"Yes, tomorrow." Carly yawned and led him down to her herb studio. Once they were inside, she placed the cup carefully on the work station and then pulled out her phone.

A moment later, Gigi answered. "Hey, Carly. Did you get it?"

"Yes. How soon can you get here?"

"I'm on my way."

Carly ended the call and grinned up at Jeremiah. "If all goes well, we'll have Liam's real identity in about an hour."

CHAPTER FOURTEEN

*J*eremiah peered into the bottom of the teacup at the sachet of herbs. "You're seriously telling me that Gigi has some sort of spell that can identify Liam?"

"Yes. That's what she said in her text." Carly sat back in her chair in her studio and closed her eyes, trying to stave off the exhaustion. The day she'd had already felt like it had gone on for a week, and there was no end in sight. "Gigi dropped the herbs off while we were at the hospital and texted me the instructions. After everything that happened tonight, I'd just about forgotten about the herbs, but when I went to make him tea, I found them on the counter and decided the sooner we try, the better."

His eyebrows rose and he leaned forward and propped his elbows on his knees. "Sneaky."

"Genius," she said, still amazed by her new friends. In the text, Gigi had told Carly that it was a new spell she'd been working on, but she was pretty sure it would work. It would take less time than hiring a private investigator. Plus, if Liam's prints weren't on file anywhere, they may never find his true identity.

"That, too," he said, leaning against the workbench. "You know, after I read about how the coven helped you find Harlow when she went missing, I knew I had to come here for help with Zane. I just had no idea how right that decision would be."

Carly was silent for a long moment as she tried to ignore the sudden pain that pierced her chest. Had he really only come because of the coven? Of course he had. Involving them was one of the first things he'd asked her to do. Why then was she harboring some sort of notion that he'd come because he wanted *her* help? That he knew she'd loved Zane and would stop at nothing to bring him home? Rationally, she knew that was probably part of it, but it just stung to have the unvarnished truth, that the coven had been his end-game, tossed in her face. "Yeah. They're pretty great," Carly agreed, her voice a little rough.

"All of you are great," he said, eyeing her with sudden concern as if he knew what she was thinking. He moved closer to her, reaching for her, but before he could connect, the doorbell rang.

"It's Gigi," Carly said, springing out of the chair and racing out of the room. The house was dark and quiet. Harlow and Lex must've gone to Harlow's room and there was no sound from Liam's room.

Once she reached the entry, she flicked on the light and flung the door open. Gigi stood on her doorstep in gray sweats and a pink sweatshirt. Her blond hair was tied up in a messy bun, and there wasn't a speck of makeup on her pretty face.

"Were you already in bed when I called?" Carly asked, grimacing. "I'm so sorry. I should've waited until the morning."

"No way," Gigi said, sweeping into the house. She had a tote bag over her shoulder and walked with purpose toward Carly's herb studio. "I wasn't in bed... yet," she called over her shoulder. "But hurry up, because Sebastian said something about meeting me in the bathtub in a half hour."

Carly felt her cheeks heat as she envisioned a bubble bath, only she and Jeremiah were the occupants, not Gigi and Sebastian. "Snap out of it, Carly," she told herself and rushed after her friend.

Gigi was already standing at Carly's workbench when Carly joined her in the herb studio. Jeremiah was standing across from her, watching as she pulled out a mortar and pestle, a white pillar candle, and another sachet of herbs.

"What do you want me to do?" she asked Gigi.

"Take these and prepare another cup of tea just like you did with the identification brew." Gigi flipped through a small notebook and stopped on a handwritten spell. She glanced up, spotted Carly staring at her, and raised both eyebrows. "We can't finish this until that tea is brewed."

"Right." Carly grabbed her electric kettle and filled it with water. It was a rapid boil model, and before Gigi glanced up from her notes again, Carly had the tea ready. "Here you go." She placed the cup in front of Gigi and took a step back, waiting to see how the spell was done.

Gigi grabbed the cup, poured the contents into Liam's used cup and then drank it all down. Without uttering even one incantation, her skin started to glow and her eyes glazed over as if she were in a trance.

"Gigi?" Carly whispered hesitantly.

But the other witch didn't respond even when the lights in the studio flickered before going out completely, plunging them into darkness.

Carly felt Jeremiah move closer to her, and when he placed his hand on her lower back, she was grateful for the contact. While she trusted that Gigi knew what she was doing, she was still anxious about what was going down in her studio. She'd never been party to a spell that put someone in a trance. What if something went wrong? Carly had no idea what to do. She mentally went through her stores of herbs, wondering if any of them would act as a neutralizer.

The candle that Gigi had placed in front of her flared to life, illuminating her. The trance-like expression had disappeared and was replaced with one of laser focus. Only Gigi wasn't focused on anyone or anything in particular. Just the space in front of her.

Carly squinted, trying to make out what Gigi might be looking at. Then a silver outline started to appear in the dim candlelight.

The silver outline shone brighter as a figure formed into one of a young woman with long, straight hair. She wore a long skirt and peasant blouse and had a crown of daisies in her hair. "Where is he?" she asked, her voice full of urgency and hope.

Gigi turned to Carly. "Where is Liam?"

"His name is William," the figure said with narrowed eyes. "Only his deadbeat father called him Liam."

"Okay, William," Gigi said patiently and turned to Carly. "Can you take us to him?"

"Sure, but he should be sleeping."

"It's fine," Gigi said with a nod. "She just needs to see him."

Carly led the way down the hall to the guest room and knocked gently. When she didn't get an answer, she peeked in to find their guest sleeping just as she suspected.

The silvery woman swept past her and stopped at Liam's

side. She smiled at him as tears rolled down her cheeks. "I miss you, baby. It's been a very long time, hasn't it?"

Liam's eyes flickered open. He blinked rapidly and then croaked out, "Mom?"

She nodded. "I'm here. Finally. I'm here."

Liam's gaze stayed fixated on her before his expression turned angry. "You promised you wouldn't leave me. Do you have any idea what happened to me after you were gone?"

She winced. "I'm sorry, baby. I was too weak. The drugs, they just…" She shook her head sadly. "They had a hold on me, and I just couldn't shake the addiction."

Liam turned his head, not looking at her, and that's when Carly noticed his eyes were filled with tears, too. "You have no idea what happened after you left. Dad was…" He didn't finish the sentence, just shook his head sadly. "Why are you here?"

"I was summoned." The woman glanced over at Gigi. "You want something from me."

"We just need to know your son's identity. He's had an accident and doesn't remember."

"William?" she asked, turning back to him. "What happened to you?"

He placed a hand on his injured shoulder. "Someone shot me. I don't know why."

"You don't remember who you are, but you remember me… and your bastard father?"

"Yes." His eyebrows drew together as he tried to concentrate. "Everything is fuzzy, but I do know you and dad. Or at least I can picture him in a small, white, two-bedroom house, somewhere in the desert."

"Twentynine Palms," she said. "Outside of Palm Springs. That's where we lived when you were a boy."

"Where we lived when you overdosed," he said, piercing her with his accusing gaze.

"Yes," she said softly. "It's the last place I saw you." Her gaze drifted over him. "You grew up to be so handsome."

He scoffed. "Because that's helped me so much. A few days ago, I was shot, and at the moment, I'm a charity case who has no idea who he is or how I came to be in this tiny town."

His mother straightened her shoulders and in a righteous tone said, "You're William Scott McSloan IV. Your great grandparents founded McSloan Old-fashioned Creamery. You're practically royalty in the southwest."

Carly's eyebrows rose. McSloan Old-fashioned Creamery? Liam's mother acted as if the company was a household name, but Carly had never heard of it.

"Royalty?" Liam scoffed. "I don't remember much, but I do remember that we lived in a shithole. I'd hardly think we were royalty."

"Your father's parents were taken advantage of and lost everything," she said with an indignant sniff. "But they were still very well respected. Your great-grandfather was honored with a parade when he passed on."

Liam stared at her as if she had two heads. "Do you think any of that matters when I grew up with no mother and an angry father who'd just as soon backhand me as say hello to me?"

She let out a startled gasp and clutched at his hand. "I'm so sorry, William. I thought a son would ease his bitterness. After the money was gone, he just sank further and further into a pit of despair. I wish I'd been stronger for you."

"So do I," he said. Then he stared right at her and said, "I've heard enough. It's time for you to go."

Carly had to agree. His mother wasn't helping him. But at

least she had provided background information on Liam that might help them trace what had happened to him.

His mother's silver outline started to fade. She pleaded for more time with her son, but when he shook his head, she faded from existence, leaving nothing but the dim moonlight to illuminate his room.

"Liam, are you all right?" Carly asked, moving to stand next to his bed.

"I'm fine. Just tired. I'm going back to sleep." He closed his eyes tightly as if he were blocking out any remaining emotions.

"Come on," Gigi said quietly. "Let's go so Liam can get some rest."

Carly and Jeremiah followed her out of the room, and Carly closed the door behind them.

"That went well," Gigi said happily.

"Well?" Carly countered. "We learned that his grandparents were swindled out of whatever success they'd had, that his mother died of an overdose, and that his father was abusive. It sounds more like a nightmare for him."

Gigi immediately sobered. "Of course you're right. I didn't mean it that way. Just that the spell worked and now you have the information you needed, right?"

Carly nodded. "Yes. Can you ask Sebastian to put someone on pulling up his history? Anything in his background that comes up as unusual?"

"I'm on it." Gigi typed something into her phone. "Just jotting down what the spirit said so I don't forget. I'll call you as soon as Sebastian has something." She gave Carly a quick hug and then hurried back home to her plans with her fiancé.

"That was... kinda intense," Carly said as she led the way back to her studio.

"Kinda?" Jeremiah asked. "I think that was way past kinda. It's not every day a ghost shows up."

Not every day, no, Carly thought, but it wasn't her first time encountering one. "It's not every day that someone conjures a spirit." She briefly wondered if she should ask Gigi about a potion that would help her summon her sister. The mere thought of that ability made Carly's heart ache. She'd do anything to spend more time with her twin.

Jeremiah draped an arm over her shoulder and pulled her into a half-hug. "You must really miss her," he said, seemingly reading her mind.

"Every day, all the time," Carly said and leaned into him. Tears prickled her eyes as they so often did when she thought about what a short time they'd had together. Instead of trying to appear strong and blinking them back, she did nothing to stop the tears from spilling down her cheeks.

"Come on," Jeremiah murmured. "Let's go tuck you into bed. It's been one hell of a long day."

Carly didn't argue. She just let him lead her out of the studio and up the stairs. Once they made it to the landing, she nodded toward the room at the end of the hall. "It's that one."

He walked with her and opened the door to the large master suite. After she entered, he stood at the door and said, "Get some sleep. I'll see you in the morning."

"Wait," Carly said. "Could you stay for a few minutes? Then I'll show you to the extra guest room."

"You have another guest room?" he asked with a smirk. "I assumed I'd crash on the couch."

Carly rolled her eyes. "Please. What kind of host do you think I am?"

"A gracious one," he said and moved into the room.

The quiet reverence of his tone made her heart swell with

affection. This was the Jeremiah she remembered from when they'd been kids. He'd always managed to make her feel special in the smallest ways. "Have a seat," she said, waving toward the loveseat that sat in front of a bay window that overlooked the sea. "I'm going to change, and then I'll be right out."

He nodded and did as she said, crossing his ankle over one knee as he got comfortable.

Carly grabbed a change of clothes and disappeared into her bathroom. When she returned to her room, her face was washed and clear of any makeup, her hair was tied up in a bun, and she was clad in her favorite flannel pajamas.

"You don't look a day over eighteen," Jeremiah said.

She sat beside him on the loveseat and shook her head. "Please. One doesn't get to be over fifty years old and not have the wrinkles to prove it."

He shrugged one shoulder. "Maybe a few, but you look just as radiant as you did back then."

Carly felt herself blush and nudged him with her shoulder, trying to be playful, but his arm came around her and he pulled her in for a sideways hug. She leaned into the gesture, loving the warmth radiating off him. "Thank you for being there for me today."

"There's no need to thank me," he said. "There was no place I'd rather be."

She glanced up at him, and their eyes met for a long moment until his gaze drifted to her mouth. Carly sucked in a small breath, waiting.

Jeremiah licked his lips and then tore his gaze away, but he didn't let her go. He just sighed and settled back into the couch. "I should probably go find that guest room."

She shook her head. "Not yet. I just… After everything that

happened today, I don't really feel like being alone. Do you mind staying?"

"Of course not," he said and tightened his grip on her. "I'll stay as long as you want me to."

Some of the tension of the day started to drain out of Carly. Then exhaustion set in again, and when she yawned, her eyes started to water.

Jeremiah stood and held his hand out to her. "You're beat. It's probably time for you to lie down before you pass out."

Carly couldn't argue. Her limbs had started to ache, and her eyelids were heavy. She took his hand and let him lead her over to her bed. When he pulled the covers down, she slid in and looked up at him. "Would it be weird if I asked you to stay in here tonight?"

He slowly shook his head. "It wouldn't be the first time we've slept in the same room."

No. It wouldn't. They'd shared a bed once before. It was the night before the accident when they'd lost Caydence and Zane. Although nothing had happened, she had woken up in his arms. And if Zane hadn't come barging in, she was certain Jeremiah was getting ready to kiss her. The memory of that entire day just made her heart ache, and her eyes misted over again. "Dammit, I never cry this much unless I'm at work and getting paid to turn on the waterworks."

Jeremiah sat down beside her, thumbed her tears away, and said, "It's still hard for me when I think of that day, too."

She gave him a shaky smile. "I just miss them both so much… and you, too."

His expression softened. "It hasn't been easy trying to stay mad at you all these years. Not to mention it wasn't fair. I think it's pretty obvious I just needed someone to blame, and you were the only target. I'm so sorry, Carly. You didn't deserve that."

She nodded and turned away, unable to process all the pain radiating off him. She had too much of her own to deal with. But when the bed dipped and his arms came around her as he spooned her from behind, she didn't pull away. She couldn't, because through his pain, there was love and compassion feeding right into her soul, soothing her in a way that his words couldn't.

Carly placed her hand over his that was resting on her belly and said, "Goodnight, Jeremiah."

He kissed her on her cheek and whispered, "Goodnight, love."

CHAPTER FIFTEEN

*E*arly snuggled into the warmth pressed up beside her and let out a contented sigh. Her eyes were still closed, and she was barely awake when Jeremiah's husky voice filled her ear.

"Good morning, gorgeous." He pressed a soft kiss to her neck just below her ear, making her entire body shiver slightly from the contact.

A small smile tugged at her lips. Jeremiah had held her the entire night. No wonder she'd slept so soundly. "Morning." She rolled over and pressed her palm to his cheek. "Thank you."

"For what, calling you gorgeous? That's not news is it?" he teased as he brushed a lock of her hair out of her eyes and let his fingers linger on her cheek for a moment.

"Not that," she chuckled. "But thanks for the compliment. I meant for staying in here last night. I know it was a lot to ask. It's appreciated."

"It's not a lot to ask. In fact, I should be thanking you. Do you have any idea how long it's been since I've woken up with a beautiful woman in my arms?" The teasing tone he'd had a moment ago was gone, replaced by a seriousness that had her eyes rivetted to him.

Carly shook her head.

"Far, far too long," he said and leaned in, barely touching his lips to hers.

Momentarily stunned, Carly didn't respond at first. But when he broke the kiss, her hand shot up and she buried her fingers in his hair, gently pulling him back down to her. This time, she kissed him. He had no such hesitation when it came to responding to her. His mouth moved over hers, warm and soft and insistent. Carly responded in kind and opened to him when his tongue sought entrance into her mouth. They tasted and licked and explored each other until Carly was breathless.

Carly was just about to wrap herself around him when he pulled back and stared down at her, his face flushed and his hair mussed. He'd never looked sexier than in that moment with his lips slightly swollen and his eyes glassy from desire. Sometime during the night, he'd lost his shirt and was clad only in his jeans. She couldn't help it when her gaze lingered on his well-formed pecs. "Why'd you stop?" she asked thickly.

He let out a low chuckle. "Because if I didn't, you'd be naked right now and I'd be buried inside of you."

"Holy hell," she breathed, ready to rip her clothes off and make that statement a reality. "And that's a problem because, why?"

Jeremiah laid down on his back and stared up at the ceiling as he let out a groan. "Maybe because William Scott McSloan IV is downstairs, and we should be focusing on finding Zane?"

Carly sat up and buried her face in her hands. What was wrong with her? Here she was acting like a hormone-riddled teenager while Zane was still missing. "Sorry. We'd better get up and get to it."

Jeremiah reached out and grabbed her hand, stopping her. "Wait."

She glanced back at him and nearly melted when he licked his lips.

"One more kiss?"

There was no way she could resist him. She nodded, her breath already coming faster with the anticipation.

He sat up, took her face in both his hands, and kissed her so thoroughly that her head was spinning when he finally released her. "We'll finish the rest of that later," he said as he got up and tugged his shirt back over his head.

Carly was still speechless when he walked out of her bedroom a moment later. She shook her head, trying to clear the lust fog from her brain. What had just happened? Had Jeremiah just made a promise that this, whatever it was, wasn't over? She pressed a hand to her chest, trying to calm her rapidly beating heart, and then dragged herself to the shower.

* * *

As Carly descended the stairs, laughter drifted from the kitchen.

Laughter?

What was there to laugh about? Zane was being held captive somewhere, Liam had nearly died, and Jeremiah... Well, she had no idea what was going on with him. Forty-five minutes ago, she'd been ready to forget everything else and finally succumb to the long-suppressed desire she had for him. It wasn't even remotely appropriate considering everything that was going on.

When she entered the kitchen, she spotted Harlow and Liam at the table. Liam had his arm in a sling to protect his shoulder, but other than that, he was looking a hundred times better than he had the night before. His scrapes and bruises were starting to fade, though he was still on the pale side.

"Morning," Harlow said, grabbing a cup and filling it with coffee. "Lex said to tell you it was nice seeing you again last night."

"It was nice to see her, too," Carly said, glancing around. "Where's Jeremiah?"

"Right here," he said from the kitchen doorway. His dark hair was wet, and his cheeks were flushed from the shower.

Harlow handed Carly the mug of coffee and held up the pot to Jeremiah. "Coffee?"

"Yes, please." He smiled at her.

Carly waved a hand, indicating he should sit at the table and then finally noticed that the table was filled with pancakes, eggs, and bacon. She glanced at Harlow. "You did all this?"

Harlow nodded. "It's not often we have guests. I thought it would be a nice way to start the day."

"That was very nice of you," Carly said, giving her niece a hug and squeezing her hand. She was grateful that whatever had been bothering Harlow the night before seemed to have passed. "Thank you."

"It's my pleasure." She dished up some food for Liam and then sat next to him. "Let me know if you need anything else."

He nodded his thanks and picked up a piece of bacon.

"Did you sleep okay?" Carly asked him as she took a seat.

"I guess," Liam mumbled.

Her further attempts to engage him in conversation were unsuccessful, and eventually she gave up on the small talk and got down to business. After retrieving her laptop from her office, she sat back down and fired it up. With her coffee cup in one hand, she typed in William Scott McSloan IV into the browser. Immediately, a couple of articles from ten years ago popped up, indicating he was a missing person.

"Jackpot," Carly whispered.

Everyone's eyes were on her as they waited for her to continue. Carly quickly scanned the article and let out a small gasp. Pointing at the line, she said, "Liam went missing from the same lake as Zane. It says here he rented a cabin, and when he went missing, all of his belongings were found in his cabin, including his wallet and identification. Even his car was still there. They conducted a week-long search, and when they found nothing, the authorities closed the case, assuming he'd drowned in a midnight swim even though there were no witnesses or traces of his disappearance."

"I went missing from the same lake as Lazer?" Liam asked, his face pinched in concentration. "How is that possible?"

"Sounds like whoever is abducting people wants it to look like their victims died, and that lake is perfect for accidents," Jeremiah said. He turned to Carly. "Look up drownings at Picture Lake and see what comes up."

Carly typed in the search. "It looks like there are anywhere from two to six drownings a year." She read through the information on her screen and then looked up at the group. "But what's more interesting are the bodies that aren't found. There's been one of those types of drownings where no body is recovered every five years for the past forty years."

"Write those names down," Jeremiah said. "We'll get a PI to run some checks and see what kind of backgrounds they had."

"Sure. Sounds like a decent idea." She eyed Liam. "I'm going to ask Sebastian to do one on you, too. See if we can get any more information. Is that all right?"

"I guess," he said, pushing the eggs around on his plate. "It's just infuriating not being able to remember anything. Why was

I at that lake? What happened that I never returned? Where was I taken?"

"Those are the things we're trying to find out," Carly reassured him. "Hopefully the information will lead us to who took you and where Zane is being held."

"Zane," he said quietly as if testing out the name. "I still think of him as Lazer."

Carly and Jeremiah shared a look. Jeremiah cleared his throat. "I know. It's okay if you use that name. We know who you mean."

"Yeah. Okay." He sighed and pushed his plate away from him. "I hate this feeling. I know the information we need is in here." He tapped his temple. "But I can't access it."

"That reminds me," Jeremiah said. "I've been wondering how you found me just from that picture Zane gave you. If he didn't give you any details, how did you track me down?"

Liam pointed at Carly. "It was her. I saw her on some old promo poster in Hollywood. When I looked her up, I found the old articles of when Lazer... I mean Zane went missing. From there it was easy to find you. I figured it would be harder to get to a movie star."

"That was lucky," Carly said. "Seeing a promotional poster, I mean."

"I guess." He closed his eyes, and Carly could almost see the exhaustion wash over him. "You're kind of everywhere, though. It was only a matter of time."

"I am?" Carly looked at Harlow for confirmation.

"I'm afraid so," Harlow said, giving her a gentle smile. "There's a reason we keep you off social media."

Carly groaned. "When are they going to get tired of writing nonsense articles about me?"

"Probably never," Harlow said. "But at least fans aren't camped outside your door... usually."

"Thank the goddess for small favors." Carly got up and started clearing the table.

"I think we should go to that lake," Liam said.

Carly turned around and found him leaning forward, his expression urgent.

"I have a feeling it will break something loose. Help me remember," Liam insisted.

"That's probably not a good idea with your shoulder—" Jeremiah started.

Liam cut him off. "My shoulder will be fine with some pain potions." He eyed Carly. "You can make those for me, right? I saw your herb studio this morning."

"Well, sure," Carly said. "But I don't want to interfere in your medical care. If your doctors think you should be on pain medication, it's better to refer to them."

"I'm not taking any opioids," Liam said forcefully and then frowned. "I don't know why, but everything inside of me is screaming no."

"But a pain potion is all right?" Carly asked with a raised eyebrow.

"Uh, yeah. I guess." Liam rubbed a hand over his eyes. "What the hell? Am I some sort of addict? Is that why I'm fiercely against opioids?"

"Could be," Jeremiah said. "Or it could just be that you're allergic. Or maybe because your mom overdosed. Whatever it is, a pain potion is better anyway. They tend to have less side effects and can be tailored for your needs. Right, Carly?"

"Right," she agreed. "But I'll need to make enough to last for the trip up there and back.."

"Is there anything I can do to help?" Harlow asked.

Carly gave her a grateful smile. "You already did it. Breakfast was amazing. Thank you."

"Sure, but I meant with finding Zane. Did you ever figure out what Enchantment means?" her niece asked.

"No." Carly shook her head. "We found a few references, but nothing that makes sense. We're going to ask Sebastian if he can dig anything up. I suppose anything that is connected to the lake or the surrounding area."

"Enchantment?" Liam asked and then frowned in frustration. "That word means something to me, I just can't put my finger on it."

"It does?" Carly and Jeremiah asked at the same time.

He nodded slowly. "I can't seem to place it. Enchantment is…" He let out a growl of frustration. "I can see Lazer standing there and hear him say the word. But I don't know why." He squeezed his eyes shut and cursed under his breath. "Why can't I remember anything?"

"It has to be a memory spell," Carly said.

"Can the coven help?" Harlow asked. "Gigi or Iris maybe? Some sort of potion to break the spell or hypnotism to try to unlock his memories?"

"I'm willing to try anything," Liam said, sounding hopeful again. "If your coven can help, I'm all for it."

"I can ask," Carly said, feeling hopeful, too. If there was one thing she'd learned, it was that the coven was badass and could do a lot more than she'd ever imagined in the spell department. She grabbed her phone and sent a group text, asking if anyone was available to brainstorm solutions.

Gigi texted back almost immediately. *I'm meeting Grace at the Point of View Café in an hour. Does that work?*

Carly quickly tapped out a reply. *I'll be there.* She looked up from her phone. "I'm going to make those pain potions and then go out to meet part of the coven for a few hours."

Liam nodded once. "Sounds like as good a plan as any. I'm going to go lay back down. Wake me if anything important happens."

"We'll leave for the lake when Carly gets back," Jeremiah said.

"Fine." Liam kept his head down as he shuffled back to the ground floor guest room.

Carly watched him leave and couldn't help the ache in her chest. The man just seemed so broken. And why wouldn't he be? The person he cared about most in the world was being held captive somewhere, a place Liam had clearly been to but couldn't remember due to a scrambled memory. Carly could think of nothing more disorienting than not knowing who she was or anything about her past. The thought sent a shiver up her spine and strengthened her resolve to find Zane and get Liam answers to what kind of life he'd had for the past ten years.

"We'll find a way to restore his memory," Jeremiah said softly from behind her. "And we'll find Zane. We won't give up until we do."

She glanced over her shoulder at him, saw the determination in his gaze, and strengthened her own resolve. "Damn straight. We're not losing Zane a second time."

Jeremiah placed a reassuring hand on her shoulder then took a step back. "I'll see what research I can dig up about Picture Lake and will be ready to take off when you get back."

"Thanks." She pressed a kiss to his cheek and disappeared into her herb studio, ready to get to work.

CHAPTER SIXTEEN

*C*arly walked into the Pointe of View Café and scanned the dining room for her friends. At first, she thought she'd missed them and felt a wave of disappointment. Those old feelings of abandonment started to set in, but she shook them off, determined not to be brought down by her past traumas. Instead, she ordered an iced coffee and then decided to take a walk through the dining room just to be sure she hadn't missed them.

As soon as she rounded a corner, she spotted not only Gigi and Grace, but Iris as well. All three were huddled in a booth with their heads down, studying some paperwork.

"He's just not being reasonable," Iris said, scribbling something on the paperwork. "He went from being a pleasant man with a dream to a tyrant who wants everything done yesterday with zero patience for city permits and public feedback on the zoning issue. I swear, if we didn't have that stupid contract he asked me to sign, I'd fire him in half a second."

Carly cleared her throat, announcing her presence to the

group. When they all looked up at her, she waved. "Hi. I almost missed you guys way back here in the corner."

Grace moved over immediately, making room for her. "Sorry. I should've texted that we were back here."

"What's going on?" Carly asked as she slid into the booth.

"Remember that mansion on the bluff overlooking the sea that I sold some months back? The one that's south of here?" Grace asked.

"Sure." Carly took a sip of her coffee. "You sold it out from under your ex. So in addition to a lovely commission, you got to stick it to him. Right?"

"That's the one," Grace said with a self-satisfied grin. The smile faded as she added, "The buyer owns a number of high-end restaurants throughout California. Pretty important in the business world apparently, but now he's giving Iris heartburn. He hired her to help him start his B&B business here in Premonition Pointe and is calling her nonstop. He even has me showing him more properties, hoping to find one that is already zoned commercial."

"Instead of the one by the sea?" Carly asked, wondering if he'd sell the mansion.

"In *addition* to the one he already owns. Apparently he wants to start a small chain." Grace shrugged. "I'm happy to do that, but he does seem a little keyed up."

"A little?" Iris asked, her eyebrows raised. "The man is driving me nuts."

Gigi patted her hand. "If anyone can wrangle him and the red tape, it's you. I swear, I've never met anyone as efficient as you are with this stuff."

"I agree," Grace said. "No one knows her stuff better than you."

Iris was the former mayor of Premonition Pointe and had a

sixth sense when it came to businesses. If someone came to her with an idea, she always knew if it would be successful. She'd recently opened up a successful consulting business to help grow Premonition Pointe. In addition, she and her boyfriend, Kade, were starting a non-profit to help new startup businesses get on their feet.

"Thanks," Iris said, closing her folder. "Enough about that. It'll work out one way or another." She focused on Carly. "Didn't Grace say you could use some coven help? What do you need?"

Carly placed her hands down on the table and said, "It's Liam. The man who was shot in front of my house. His memory is scrambled, almost as if he's been spelled, and I'm wondering if there's anything we can do about it. If it is a spell, can we reverse it?"

Everyone turned to look at Gigi, who chewed on her bottom lip before she met Carly's gaze. "We could try a memory spell."

Carly couldn't help the shiver that ran up her spine. "The last time I tried one of those, I ended up aging so fast I thought I was headed straight for the casket."

"That won't happen if you have the power of the coven behind you," Grace said. "But I'm not sure a memory spell is the right way to handle this anyway. All of the ones I've read about work more like an amplifier. They're to recall current memories in more detail. But I seriously doubt one will combat someone else's magic."

Gigi nodded. "I agree. It would take a powerful spell to wipe out someone's memories. Very powerful. We'd need to reverse it. And it would likely take all of us." She pursed her lips as she thought. "I'd like to see if Hope could hear any of his thoughts. See what's really going on in his head before we do anything."

"Hope is over at Lucas's shop today, working on his monthly open house," Grace said. "I can give her a call and see if she has some time to help us out."

"Anyone know where Joy is?" Iris asked.

Everyone shook their heads.

"I just saw her over at Liminal Space Day Spa," Skyler, Gigi's neighbor and the owner of the boutique Sky's the Limit, said as he walked toward them, a grin on his face. He placed a hand on Gigi's shoulder. "You ladies look fabulous today."

"Thanks, Sky," Gigi said, smiling up at him. "You saw Joy at the spa?"

He nodded. "She was just about finished getting her hair done." He held his hands out for inspection, showing off his sparkling blue fingernails. "I got a long-overdue massage and then a manicure. Isn't this color fabulous?"

Gigi sighed. "How is it that your nails are nicer than mine?"

"It's because you spend all your time making fabulous skin care products and potions. It's hell on the hands." He turned his attention to Carly. "That reminds me, I'm going to need another batch of your miracle cellulite cream soon. You know how hard it is to keep it in stock."

Carly groaned. "I'm sorry. My life has been a little overwhelming lately. Can I get it to you next week?"

Skyler frowned. "I'll be out by then, but if it's the best you can do... then it's the best you can do."

"Carly has a couple of unexpected houseguests this week," Gigi said, patting his arm to soothe him.

"Maybe when this is over, we should consider that production facility again," Carly said to Gigi. Right after Skyler had opened his shop, they'd talked about a production facility for their products, but then Premonition Pointe had been cursed and everything had stopped while the coven helped Iris save the town. And now Carly was preoccupied with finding Zane. She hadn't thought about her cream or the idea of the production facility since the day Jeremiah had walked back into her life.

"I like that idea," Gigi said. "My house is getting overrun with facial products. But we can talk about that later. Right now we need to work on helping Liam get his memory back. Can someone call Hope and Joy? Maybe we can all meet at Carly's and see what we can do."

"Who's Liam?" Skyler asked, glancing around as if the man in question would appear out of nowhere.

"The man who was shot in front of Carly's house a few days ago," Grace explained. "We think his memory has been magically wiped, so we're trying to help."

"Oh, wow." Skyler's eyes widened. "Intrigue. Anything I can do to help?"

"Yes," Carly said. "He doesn't have any clothes. Can you bring him some from your shop? New or used. Doesn't matter. I'll pay for them."

"Sure. But I'll need his measurements."

"Can you come by the house?" Carly asked, even as she internally cringed. She was inviting practically everyone she knew to the house even though they were supposed to be leaving for Picture Lake. But if the coven could retrieve Liam's memory, that would be better than snooping around the lake. She had to try. And inviting Skyler was just practical. Liam didn't have any clothes of his own and had been wearing the same sweats since they'd left the hospital. "He's still recovering from the bullet wound, and we're not sure it's safe for him to be seen in public right now. We don't know if someone is still looking for him."

"I'll grab some stuff from the shop, and he can try them on. Can you give me a verbal description? Approximate height and weight would do it," Skyler said, already pulling out his phone so he could take notes.

"Um, tall and lanky," Carly said. "Maybe six feet. I'd guess no more than one eighty."

Skylar nodded. "That's enough. Unless you have any idea on shoe size."

That she did know, but only because her security guard had said his spare shoes fit Liam perfectly. "Men's eleven."

"On it." He tucked his phone back into his pocket. "I'll go now and meet you at your house."

"Thank you," she said, more than grateful. How had she gotten so lucky to find friends like the ones in Premonition Pointe who were going out of their way to help her?

Skyler squeezed her hand briefly. "Anything for you, doll." He winked and strode out of the café.

"Both Hope and Joy are headed to your house," Grace said, holding her phone up to show the latest text string. "We should probably get going if we want to meet them there."

"Okay," Carly said, somewhat amazed that everyone had jumped into action. She was used to Hollywood types trying to please her, but that was always transactional. She could be certain they'd want something from her in the end. What was remarkable about this group was that she knew they were doing it because they cared about her and not because they wanted anything in return. She wondered if she'd ever stop being surprised by their fierce friendship. She hoped so, but prayed she'd never take them for granted.

As they walked out of the café, Carly paused and said, "If I forget to say it later, thank you. Just thank you."

"We haven't done anything yet," Gigi said, squeezing her hand as she smiled at her friend. "Wait to see what kind of results we get before you thank us."

Carly shook her head. "No. Even if nothing works, I want you to know I appreciate all of you. More than you know."

Grace came up and gave her a tight hug. "We love you, Carly, and it's not because you throw fancy parties with famous people, either."

"Yeah, that's just a perk," Gigi teased.

Iris rolled her eyes. "Celebrities are overrated."

Carly slipped out of Grace's embrace and snorted a laugh. "No truer words were ever spoken. Thanks again, everyone."

They all waved off her gratitude, indicating it was no big deal, and then they followed her back to her house by the sea.

CHAPTER SEVENTEEN

"I thought we were headed to Picture Lake," Jeremiah said into Carly's ear as he stared at all the women gathered in her living room. Hope and Joy had already arrived when she and the rest of the coven got there.

"We were, and we still can if this doesn't work," Carly said. "But the coven was free now, so I figured we'd try to break the spell that's making Liam forget his past. If it works, we won't need to go to the lake, right? And if it doesn't, Gigi is going to research other ways to access his memory."

Jeremiah stuffed his hands in his pockets and nodded. "Makes sense. What can I do?"

"I don't know yet." Carly turned to him and placed both hands on his chest as she looked up at him. "I really think this might work, though. And it feels like we're getting close to finding Zane."

He brushed a thumb over her cheek, giving her a half-hearted smile. "As much as I want to believe that, let's not get ahead of ourselves. One step at a time."

Carly knew he was just managing his own expectations.

Honestly, it's what she should do as well, but she just had a feeling that they were getting really close. That today might give them the clues they needed to find Zane. She cupped his cheek and nodded. "You're right, one step at a time."

Jeremiah took her hand in his and walked with her over to where the coven members were gathered and discussing what spell they wanted to try.

"I thought I was here to eavesdrop on his thoughts," Hope said. She was leaning against the stairwell banister, and she looked chic in her tight jeans, oversized sweater, and knee-high black boots. Her dark curls perfectly framed her face, making Carly slightly envious of her natural good looks. She looked like the type of woman who could roll out of bed and be ready in five minutes while still looking fabulous. Carly had to work a lot harder than that and always had. Her classic features only got her so far.

"Yes, of course," Carly said when Jeremiah nudged her because she hadn't responded. "Let's go see if he's awake." She gestured for Hope to follow her and told the others to send Skyler in when he arrived.

With Hope right behind her, Carly knocked on Liam's door.

"Come in," he called.

Carly pushed the door open to find him sitting in one of the chairs near the window and staring out at the ocean. "Hey. I wanted to introduce you to my friend, Hope. She's one of my coven members."

Hope walked right over to him and sat in the matching chair. She held her hand out. "It's nice to meet you, Liam."

He hesitated but then shook his head before clasping his hand over hers. "Are you here to do some sort of memory spell?"

"Actually, I'm here to try to read your mind." She flashed him a smile.

He blinked at her and then let out a breath as he leaned back into his chair. "Seriously? You can do that?"

"Sometimes," she said with a shrug. "I try not to, because honestly, I don't want to know what people are actually thinking. Especially if it's about me." She paused and eyed him. Then she cackled. "Funny."

He chuckled along with her. It was the first time Carly had heard him laugh. She placed a hand over her heart, hoping she'd hear it again sometime soon. She hated seeing and feeling so much of his pain.

"What were you thinking?" Carly asked him.

"Nothing. Just wanted to see if she was for real." Liam's laughter had faded, but his smile was still there.

"He was thinking that if I had blue eyeshadow and red hair dye, that I'd look just like Endora from *Bewitched*. And you know what? I can kind of see it," she said, cackling again.

"You remember the TV show *Bewitched*?" Carly asked him.

He shrugged. "It's weird, right? I remember a bunch of shows that I know are from my childhood, but I have no memory of actually watching them."

"That's very interesting," Hope said. "Very interesting."

"Why?" Carly and Liam asked at the same time.

"I think it implies that your memory has actually been suppressed by some spell instead of just wiped clean," she said. "That's good news, as we can usually reverse spells. What we can't do is make a memory form out of thin air."

"There are definitely memories locked in there," Liam said as he averted his gaze. "I can feel it. I just can't seem to latch onto them."

Hope studied him for a long moment before she said, "You remember him though, don't you?"

"Him?" Carly asked, but both of them ignored her.

Liam nodded. "I see him in my mind all the time. I just can't ever place him anywhere. The background is fuzzed out. It's just him, standing there in my thoughts asking for me to find him."

Carly's heart nearly broke in two. She had to turn away to keep him from seeing the tears that welled in her eyes again. Normally she wasn't this overly emotional, but lately she couldn't seem to keep her tears under control. She cleared her throat and forced herself to turn back around when she said, "That's why the coven is here. We're going to find him. I promise you that we won't give up until we have him home."

It was his turn to study her. Carly stood exactly where she was with her chin held high, letting the determination filter through her, letting it strengthen her resolve.

"You know, if anyone else had said that, I'd probably roll my eyes or just say, 'Sure, Jan,'" Liam said with a half-grin. "But from you? I believe you."

"She could be acting," Hope said. "I hear she's some sort of accomplished actress."

Liam chuckled for the second time that day. "She's good, but not that good."

Carly laughed, loving that he wasn't taking her profession too seriously. Far too many people did.

"Hello, hello," Skyler called as he poked his head around the open door. "Look out, because everyone's favorite fairy godfather is here."

"Who?" Liam asked, confused. "Fairy godfather?"

"That's right." Skyler was holding multiple garment bags as

he swept into the room. "I'm the guy who's going to dress you in something better than those gray sweatpants."

"What's wrong with gray sweatpants?" Liam asked, looking down at his bottom half.

"Nothing," Skyler said with a smirk. "Not unless you're trying to be a walking thirst trap."

"What's that?" Liam asked while Hope laughed.

"Oh, sweet baby Jesus," Skyler said, his eyes flashing with amusement. "You're such an adorable baby gay, aren't you?"

"Uh…" Liam glanced away as his cheeks flushed bright pink. "I'm not sure what that means, but I doubt I'm a *baby* gay."

"If you say so." Skyler snickered. "Definitely adorable." Then he sobered. "Okay, let's see what fits." He shooed Hope and Carly out of the room. "Boys only for this one, girls. Liam's been gawked at enough."

Carly led Hope out of the room and closed the door behind her. "Did you hear anything useful?"

"Not really." Hope frowned. "His mind is full of images of Zane. He's scared for him and frustrated that he can't remember anything about their life together, only that they had one."

"I can imagine. At least we now know that his memories are there for sure, right?" Carly asked.

"Yeah." Hope said. "I just don't know if we can break through that spell without causing damage."

Carly froze. It was obvious Liam was in love with Zane, and she had to assume that the feeling was mutual if Zane helped Liam escape their situation. The last thing she wanted to do was cause harm, especially to the man Zane loved. "We can't let that happen," she said firmly. "Under no circumstances can we let any more harm come to Liam."

"I agree." Hope slipped her arm through Carly's. "The man has been through enough. But I don't know how much of that we can control if someone is still after him."

"We'll just have to get to the bad guys first," Carly said with grim determination. "Come on. Let's go talk to the rest of the coven and see if they have any ideas on how to break this spell."

Hope nodded, and together they joined the rest of the coven, who'd moved outside to the deck.

"I think our best shot is a reversal spell," Gigi said. "That way it won't react with the one he's already cursed with."

"But we don't know what spell was used," Iris said. "Don't we need to know exactly how it was cast in order to remove it?"

"Not necessarily." Joy pushed a lock of her long blond hair out of her eyes. "We could try a general reversal spell."

Grace shook her head. "It's stronger than that. Can't you feel how sticky it is? We'd need more than a general reversal, I think."

"I could call on my spirits and see if they have any insight," Gigi offered. "They sometimes know stuff or can find things out. Like a spirit network of sorts."

"That's probably the best idea," Carly said, stepping closer. "It's the least invasive way to start."

"Carly and I are worried that breaking the spell will harm Liam. Considering his current health, it's probably best to be as cautious as possible," Hope said.

Grace nodded. "It's settled then. We'll call in Gigi's spirits first to see if they can offer any insight and then we'll go from there."

With everyone in agreement, they retreated back into the

house just in time to hear a blood curdling scream, followed by a series of gunshots.

Carly was tackled to the floor and started to struggle until she heard Jeremiah's voice in her ear.

"It's me, Carly," he said. "Just be still until security says otherwise."

She did as he asked while frantically scanning her home, desperate to make sure her friends hadn't been hurt. They were all on her floor, their hands covering their heads.

"Stay down. Nobody move until I say so," she heard Jake call to them.

Footsteps pounded on her wood floors, followed by another gunshot and a loud thunk as someone hit the floor.

Carly's entire body was sparking with magic as her fight instinct kicked in.

"Jake's down," Hope called as Carly spotted Gigi and Grace both getting to their feet. Magic was sparking at the ends of their fingertips. Carly pushed at Jeremiah, desperate to get to Jake, the man who'd been protecting her for years. "Let me up. I have to help them."

"No," he said, clasping his hand over hers. "It's not safe."

The rest of the coven had gotten to their feet and were moving forward, all of them with determined expressions on their faces.

"I. Don't. Care." Carly swiftly twisted and rolled out from underneath him. After scrambling to her feet, she glanced around, looking for Jake. He was lying face down on her floor, unmoving. Her throat tightened as she held off a scream. He had to be okay. He just had to.

She took off toward him but then froze when she saw who the coven was circling, unable to believe her eyes. "Zane?" she whispered, horror filling every inch of her body. "What are you doing?"

He was holding Liam, shielding himself with a gun pressed to Liam's side. "It's Lazer," he growled. "Zane is dead."

But there was no mistaking Zane. Carly would know him anywhere. He had the same eyes with a scar just over his left eyebrow. The birthmark on his neck. The dragon tattoo on his forearm that he'd had a friend ink on him when he was just sixteen years old. "No. You're not," Carly said calmly. "You're miraculously alive. After all these years, we've finally found you. Or you've found us."

Zane's gaze bored into hers. His expression was cold, void of any emotion. "I'm only here for Liam. It's time for him to come back home."

Carly's gaze drifted to Liam's. There were tears in his eyes, but he didn't look broken. His expression was full of determination.

"I'm going with him," Liam said firmly. "There's no point in trying to stop us."

"Neither of you have to go anywhere," Carly said, surprised at the strength in her voice. Inside, she was terrified, and her heart was breaking at the scene in front of her. But there was no time to fall apart. She could grieve for her friend later. Right now, her priority was to save Liam. She would not let any more harm come to him. "Why don't you put the gun down," she said to Zane. "No one wants to harm anyone here. Liam's even said he'd go with you willingly."

"I know he will," Zane said, closing his eyes very briefly as he pressed a kiss to Liam's temple. "This is to keep you all in line."

"Zane," Jeremiah said in a calm, even tone. "I don't know what's going on or where you've been all these years, but I do know *you*. This thing you're doing? It's not you. I know that. Why don't you put the gun down and we'll work this all out? You'll come home and we'll start over. Put all these years behind us."

Carly had to admire Jeremiah's effort, but she could see that nothing they said was going to change anything.

Zane's hold tightened on Liam as his eyes narrowed in his brother's direction. "You're right. You don't know anything about what I've been through. And the idea that I can just come home is laughable. Make the witches step back, or else someone is going to get hurt." His gaze flickered back to Carly when he said, 'someone is going to get hurt,' making it clear he meant her.

"Zane," Carly said, trying to block out the pain that pierced her heart. "We love you. Don't do this."

"You don't understand," he said. "I don't have a choice." His voice broke on the word *choice*, making Carly certain that whatever was happening there in her living room, Zane was being forced into it. She knew that she could be deluding herself by not believing that her old friend was capable of such a horrendous crime, but she really didn't think so. The coldness in his gaze had vanished and been replaced by despair.

"If you hurt Carly, it will be the last thing you ever do," Jeremiah threatened and took a step forward.

Zane jerked Liam and pressed the gun in closer to his side, making Liam yelp with pain while Carly grabbed Jeremiah's arm, stopping him from advancing.

The coven was frozen, watching and waiting for a signal. But with the gun trained on Liam, Carly had no idea what they could do to stop the horror in front of them.

"Hands in the air where I can see them," Zane ordered.

No one moved.

"Do it now!" Zane's voice boomed through the house as he brought the gun up to Liam's temple. There were tears in Zane's eyes, and Carly felt that he was on the verge of losing control. The mix of horror and guilt streaming from him was so strong that it nearly brought her to her knees.

Carly started to raise her hands and softly said, "Do as he says."

Everyone eyed her, clearly not wanting to go down without a fight.

"Please," she pleaded.

Relief flashed in Zane's eyes before he glanced at the old grandfather clock against her wall. The time kicked over to noon, and the bells started to chime. He whispered something in Liam's ear.

The other man nodded once and then started to chant. "Let time take us back to the place we belong." As he continued to chant the words, magic poured from Carly's clock, the chimes got louder, and suddenly the pair disappeared into thin air, leaving nothing in the place where they'd stood except a black business card that floated silently in the air.

Carly ran forward and grabbed it. After flipping over both sides, she glanced up to find everyone staring at her.

"What does it say?" Jeremiah asked.

She held it up. "Just one word. *Enchantment.*"

CHAPTER EIGHTEEN

*A*fter stuffing the business card into Jeremiah's hands, Carly ran over to Jake and dropped to her knees to check on her bodyguard. "Jake?" she cried, running her hands over him, searching for a wound. "Where were you shot?"

He didn't move or make a sound. She scanned his body for any signs of blood but found none. What the hell was going on? She pressed her fingertips to his pulse and was relieved to find his heart was definitely still beating.

"Look," Hope said, standing over her. "There, embedded in his shoulder. It looks like a dart."

Carly scanned him again, her focus narrowing in on the dark blue dart. "Tranquilizer?" she asked.

"It looks like it." Grace kneeled down and inspected the dart. "We should be careful to not disturb any prints."

"I'll call Sebastian," Gigi said.

Carly pulled her phone out and called the security company to explain what happened. After they assured her backup staff was on their way, she ran into the guest room, finding that Skyler had also been hit with a tranquilizer dart.

He was crumpled on the floor with a blazer clutched in his hands.

"Where the hell are Phil and Mikey?" she muttered to herself.

"Phil is outside in the van, also unconscious from a dart," Jeremiah said. "They found Mikey in the same condition outside on the deck."

Carly stood and walked right into his arms, burying her face in his chest. He pulled her close and murmured that everything would be all right.

She tilted her head to look up at him. "You do realize that Zane didn't want to be doing any of that, right?"

He scoffed. "I think you're reaching. My brother isn't the man we both remember."

"Yes, he is," Carly insisted and took a step back. "Just look at the evidence. He had a gun. A real one. That was most definitely a Glock he had trained on Liam. And he fired it at least twice, though as far as I can tell, he had no intention of actually shooting anyone. I heard those shots. Didn't you?"

"Of course, I heard them. What I don't understand is who he was shooting at or why it was necessary if he was using tranq darts on people."

"Exactly," Carly said. "It seems obvious to me that he didn't want to shoot anyone, and that the Glock was just for show."

Jeremiah scoffed. "You don't think he'd have shot Liam?"

"No. I don't," Carly said with certainty. "But he needed to make it look good. Which implies someone was watching or at least listening to him."

"You think someone was watching that go down?" Jeremiah spun and strode out of the room, presumably to check to see if anyone was still watching the house.

Carly started to follow, but then she heard Skyler moan.

She ran over to his side and pressed a hand to his chest to keep him from moving as his eyes fluttered open.

"What the hell happened? I feel like I just woke up after a bender," he croaked out.

"You were shot with a tranquilizer dart." She eyed the dart still in his shoulder. That needed to come out before he got up off the floor. She glanced around the room, and spotted what she needed on the nightstand. After grabbing a tissue, she used it to pluck the dart out of his shoulder and carefully placed it on the dresser.

"Son of a bitch," Skyler said, rubbing the area that had been hit. "That hurts like hell."

"I'm so sorry." She squeezed his hand. "I have no idea how he got past security and into the house without anyone noticing."

Skyler rubbed the back of his neck and frowned. "Where's Liam? And that guy he let in?"

Carly's eyes widened. "Liam let someone in?"

He nodded. "Through the back door. Dark headed guy. About your age. He was in black jeans and a green Army jacket."

"Zane," she breathed. "Liam let him in." She gritted her teeth. Was it all some sort of setup? But that didn't make any sense. They didn't take anything except Liam. And Zane had even left some sort of clue. She stood by her theory that Zane didn't want to hurt anyone. Using a tranq gun saw to that. It wasn't as if he'd tried to run anyone off the road or actually shot someone, like when they'd shot Liam outside of her house. This was *different*.

"Liam called him Lazer, I think." Skyler rubbed at his forehead. "Dear baby Jesus, this splitting headache is going to kill me."

Carly helped him up and led him into the kitchen where she supplied a large glass of water and some ibuprofen.

"Think I could trouble you for a couple of those?" Jake asked, sitting next to Skyler at her table.

"Of course." Carly handed him the bottle and watched as he downed two of them with a bottle of water.

"I'm sorry, Ms. Preston," he said, as he handed back the medication bottle. "The security break here today was completely unacceptable. We'll run a thorough check of all security footage and test the alarm system at every entry point for failures. We should have a report for you by tomorrow. In the meantime, the boss has called in reinforcements so that we'll have someone watching from every angle until we determine the breech."

"I know how he got in," Skyler said.

Jake turned to him. "You do?"

Skyler nodded and proceeded to tell him how Liam had excused himself to go to the bathroom. Skyler followed a moment later, intending to get something to drink, but then he spotted Liam letting Zane in through a door at the end of the hall that led to the back deck. "Zane came in with a gun in both hands. I hightailed it back into the guestroom, but he followed and the next thing I knew, I was waking up with the mother of all hangovers."

"Did Liam know he was coming?" Carly asked.

"I have no idea," Skyler said. "It kind of seemed like it because he left the room at that exact time, but I suppose Zane could've just been waiting for his chance."

"It's likely that the visit was planned, but things went sideways when the house was full of people," Jake said. "It would explain why it all went down the way it did. He carefully took out Phil and Mikey before entering the house, so obviously he did his homework. It's unclear if Liam knew about it in advance."

Something had been niggling at the back of Carly's mind, and at that moment she realized she hadn't seen her niece since she'd been home. She jumped up and moved into the living room. "Has anyone seen Harlow?"

They all shook their heads.

Carly ran upstairs while simultaneously dialing her niece's number on her cell phone. The call went straight to voice mail. "Dammit." Carly left a quick message asking her to call as soon as possible. She knocked swiftly on her door before barging in. The room was completely empty.

Dread swirled in Carly's gut and then moved upward, spiraling around her and making her chest ache. Something was very wrong. She could just feel it all the way to her bones. Carly left Harlow's room and then searched the rest of the upstairs.

Nothing.

She pulled out her phone and tried Harlow again. It still went straight to voice mail.

Flashbacks of the night that Harlow was abducted started to swirl in her mind. Her breathing quickened, and her skin turned cold as she started to shake slightly.

Panic attack.

She knew the signs, although she hadn't had one in years. Not even after Harlow had been taken the first time. Later, Carly had realized it was because she'd been in fight mode the entire time. There'd been no room to panic. She focused on her phone, doing her best to ward off all her distress.

If Harlow wasn't answering her phone, maybe her friends could help. She ran back downstairs to find Grace, who was sitting on the couch, brainstorming with Hope, Joy, and Gigi about how to trace Liam and Zane through the magical signature they'd left behind. Iris was on the phone talking to someone from the Magical Task Force. It was a government agency that investigated crimes involving the paranormal. She ignored all of it though and made a beeline for Grace.

"I need Lex's number. It's important," Carly said.

Grace didn't hesitate or question her. She just rattled it off, and Carly typed it into her phone, praying that Lex would answer.

"Hello?" Lex answered tentatively.

"Lex, it's Carly Preston. Is Harlow with you, or do you know where she is?"

"Um, no. I haven't heard from her today. Have you tried Sarah?"

"Sarah who?" Carly asked, trying to rack her brain for someone Harlow knew by that name.

"Um, Sarah Beckers? Her... um, friend?" Lex's voice went up an octave, making her statement sound like a question.

"Her friend?" Carly asked. "You seem uncertain about that."

"Well, they are definitely friends. Close friends."

Carly frowned, frustrated by the conversation. "Listen, Lex. Something went down here today at the house, and I'm frightened for Harlow's safety. If there's something you're not saying, please, just spit it out. I'm very worried about her."

"What? Omigod. Okay, Sarah is Harlow's girlfriend. I know she was working her way up to telling you, but I guess she hasn't gotten around to it yet."

"Girlfriend?" Carly shook her head. She'd suspected that Harlow might like Lex after seeing them together the other day, but she hadn't suspected that she might be dating someone else. She also didn't understand why Harlow hadn't just told her. Carly didn't care who people loved, only that they were respectful and treated each other well.

"She was nervous. I told her that given your public stance on LGBTQ plus issues, that she didn't have anything to worry about, but everyone has their own journey in coming out to those they love. I'm sorry it was me that told you and not her. I'd never do that to someone normally. But if she's in danger, then I just... You needed to know."

"Thank you, Lex. Do you have Sarah's number or know how I might get in touch with her?" Carly asked.

"Yes. Give me a sec." There was a muffled sound on the other end of the connection before she came back on and recited the number. "If you can't get a hold of her, call me back. Sarah is Bronwyn's best friend. I'll get in touch with Bron. She might know how to find her."

"You and Harlow are both dating best friends?" Carly asked stupidly as if that mattered at all.

"Yeah." She chuckled. "It's been interesting. That's why Harlow and I have been hanging out a lot. We get together when Sarah and Bron are doing bestie things."

Well at least that explained the closeness. If Carly wasn't so worried about Harlow, she'd have been overjoyed at the news. But at the moment she had more pressing matters. "Thank you, Lex. I appreciate it."

Once she ended the call, she immediately called Sarah.

"Hello?" a woman answered, her greeting full of warmth.

"Is this Sarah?" Carly asked.

"It sure is. Who's this?"

Carly introduced herself, and after a moment of Sarah stumbling over her words and gushing about how she'd been dying to meet Harlow's aunt, Carly cut her off. "Have you seen Harlow? It's an emergency."

"No. We're not supposed to meet up until tonight. Is she okay?" Sarah asked, her voice suddenly full of concern.

"I honestly don't know. There's been an incident here at the house, and now she's missing. She could just be out, but I doubt it. Her security was here on the premises. If you hear from her, can you have her call me as soon as possible? It's important."

"Of course... and Ms. Preston?" she asked.

"Yeah?"

"Will you call me if you hear anything?" her voice trembled with the request.

"Sure, honey." Carly ended the call and stared helplessly out at the ocean. Harlow never left without her security. It had been pure desperation on her part to think that maybe she was with Lex or Sarah. Mikey never would've let her leave unaccompanied.

"Carly?" Jeremiah said from right behind her.

She straightened her shoulders, determined to keep it together, and turned around to face him. "Yeah?"

He strode to her. "Everything's clear outside. If someone was watching the house, they're gone now."

She nodded and dug her fingernails into her palms to keep from screaming at the universe.

"Hey," he said softly. "What's happening right now? You look really pale, like you might pass out."

"Have you seen Harlow?" she asked instead of answering him.

"Harlow? No." He shook his head. "Not since before you left to meet your coven members at the café. I actually thought she was upstairs."

"She's not. I checked already," Carly said, knowing her voice was far too high and panicked to fool anyone into thinking she wasn't worried. "She didn't leave when I was at the café, did she?" It was one last attempt to try to convince herself that her niece hadn't been taken against her will.

"If she did, she didn't say anything to me," he said. "Though I was on the computer most of the time, trying to research strange happenings at Picture Lake. And Mikey was here, right?"

"Yes," she said quietly. "I'm really worried that she was abducted. If she was, we have zero leads or any ideas of why or where she was taken."

"But why would anyone take her?" Jeremiah asked. "She didn't know Zane and only just met Liam."

"I have no idea, but she's missing and her guard was attacked. What else am I supposed to think?"

He was silent before just pulling her in for a hug. Carly wrapped her arms around him, grateful for the moment of support.

"I did some research while you were out," he said quietly. "I found out that a handful of people who went missing from the lake eventually turned up. One just a few months after he went missing, but most of them a year or two later. What's interesting is that none of them remembered anything from the time they were lost on the lake until the time they were found."

"Just like Liam? No memory at all?" she asked, her heart pounding rapidly as she looked up at him. "That couldn't be a coincidence, could it?"

"Exactly like Liam. I have their names." He pulled a small notebook from his back pocket. "I've already called Sebastian. He's going to run a check on them all and see if they ever remembered anything."

"That sounds like a plan." She pressed her face against his chest, needing one more moment of contact.

He ran a soothing hand down her back and kissed her temple before saying, "It's still possible Harlow will turn up. She could've just slipped out for a bit, taken a walk on the beach or something."

He wasn't wrong. Harlow did tend to go for walks on the beach without telling Mikey. It was a bone of contention between them often. Unfortunately, everything inside of her was screaming that something had happened to her niece. And if there was one thing Carly knew, it was to never ignore that type of feeling.

"Carly?" Joy called as she strode up to them.

"Yeah?" She turned to her coven member and felt her heart sink when she saw Joy's face. "What's wrong? What did you find?"

She held up an iPhone with a sparkling blue case. Harlow's phone. "We found this outside on the back patio with this underneath it." She produced a small black card. One that looked exactly like the one Zane had left behind with the word *Enchantment* scrawled across it.

Carly could barely breathe as reality sank in. She clutched Joy's hand. "They have her. Whoever has Zane and Liam has Harlow. I know it."

Joy swallowed hard. "That's what I think, too."

Carly took a step back, intending to grab a framed picture of her and Harlow off the wall. "Can you try to see if you can get a vision?" She'd done it before when Harlow was abducted a few months earlier. "Please?"

"I already tried," Joy said, her voice deflated. "I'm sorry, Carly. I'll keep trying, but it's just not working."

Carly squeezed her eyes shut and willed herself not to scream. Finally she just said, "I can't lose her."

"You won't," Jeremiah said, clutching her hand. "Those cards mean something. One way or another, we'll find out what, and then we'll bring all three of them home."

Carly stared up at him, wishing with everything she had that he was right. Because if he wasn't, she was certain it'd break her.

"He's right, Carly. We won't give up. The entire coven is here for you," Joy said.

Carly shifted her gaze between the two of them, taking in their steadfast resolve. "All right." She nodded decisively. "Then let's get to work because we have no time to waste."

CHAPTER NINETEEN

*C*arly stood in the middle of her living room and felt disconnected from all the activity. Her house had turned into a bustling command station of people working hard to find not only Harlow, but Liam and Zane too. She should have been energized by everyone doing their best to trace her niece and the two men who'd disappeared from her home. Instead, she was restless and unsure of how to be useful.

Iris was pacing back and forth in front of the fireplace, still speaking with an agent from the Magical Task Force. She gave the agent Carly's address and started describing everything that had gone down in the last hour.

Joy stood near a credenza that was filled with photographs. She kept picking different ones up and closing her eyes, clearly trying to force a vision.

Jeremiah was sitting at the table with Skyler, Gigi, and Sebastian. Sebastian was a lawyer with access to private detectives, and he was making notes on everything that needed to be investigated.

Hope and Grace were huddled on the couch, discussing the spell Liam had chanted right before he and Zane disappeared.

That spell. Zane had made Liam use a timekeeper spell. A memory from when they were kids surfaced.

"Come look at this, Carly," Zane said, pointing to a page in the spell book he'd found in a used bookstore.

She was sitting at her grandmother's desk and had just finished scanning the apartment rentals in Los Angeles for when she moved after graduation. "You're not even a witch," she said, smirking.

"I might be." The mock defiance in his gaze made her laugh. "Listen, if this old coot who wrote this book can make spells happen using time, then so can I."

"Sure, Zane." Carly rose and moved to sit next to him on the loveseat, eyeing the spell. "Let's give it a try."

He raised an eyebrow. "You're down with this?"

"Sure. Why not?" She nudged him with her shoulder. "Show me what ya got, witch boy."

"Witch boy?" He wrinkled his nose. "Can't I be a mysterious wizard or something?"

"Only if you wear a velvet cloak and rename yourself something like Xanadu."

He cackled. "Do I have to wear roller skates, too?"

"With a leotard under the cape." She scanned his lanky body. "You'd look hot in tights."

"Oh god." He snorted as he threw his head back, laughing. "Can you imagine?"

"I'm trying not to," she said, gasping for air through her own laughter. "But I do see you with a headband and legwarmers."

"That's an image." He was still chuckling when he went back to reading the spell. He looked across the room and squinted. "Does that old grandfather clock still work?"

"Nope." Carly got up and strode over to the old thing. "The

pendulum stopped one day, and no one has ever done anything to repair it."

Zane appeared beside her, and peered at the old timekeeper. "The spell only works if the clock is ticking."

"Guess we're out of luck then. Cause I have no idea how to fix it," Carly said.

"Aww, come on. Don't give up so easily." He opened the glass door and started poking around the inside.

"I don't think—" Carly started to tell him that the clock was special to her grandmother and they shouldn't mess with it, but before she could get the words out, the inside of the clock started to glow. Magic rippled through the air and clung to Zane, making his skin take on the same golden hue that was coming from the clock.

Zane's eyes were wide with surprise and then determination as he started to read the spell from his book. "One of three and three of one, let time carry me until I've found my space. By thy own will, may it be done."

The magic crackled and sparked.

"It's working!" Zane said excitedly as his entire body started to glow with the magic.

Then suddenly the light vanished, and the clock started to tick again.

"Hey! You fixed the clock," Carly said, sort of in awe. She hadn't expected him to actually be able to call magic, much less do anything with it. "That's impressive."

"It didn't work," he said, frowning.

"What do you mean?" Carly gestured to the clock. "It's even set at the right time. Whatever you just did, I think it's brilliant."

"That's not what I was trying to do," he said. "Look, Car. The spell is supposed to transport people through space. I was trying to have the spell transport me outside as a test."

"You're kidding." She peered at the spell again, reading the description. *"Holy shit, dude. Seriously, you thought doing a spell to transport you through space was a good idea? What if part of you was left behind? I mean, how would that work if you lost an important appendage?"*

Both of their gazes went straight to his crotch.

Zane shifted uncomfortably and said, "Stop staring at my goods."

"I wasn't staring," she insisted, even though she totally had been. How could she not after that statement?

"You were." He rolled his eyes. "Never mind. It didn't work anyway."

"Let's try it again." Carly was a lot more interested now that she knew what the spell was supposed to do. If it meant avoiding traffic and popping in and out of places with a snap of her fingers, she was a thousand percent on board.

"I suppose two is better than one," he said and grabbed her hand. "We need to stare into the guts of the clock and envision where we want to go."

"You wanted to try outside, right? How about the porch swing?" she asked.

He nodded. "Sounds good. Now think about the swing, and together we'll recite the spell."

For the next hour, they tried the spell over and over again, but the magic didn't return. The glow had vanished, and no matter how many times they chanted the spell, there wasn't even a hint of magic.

"Well, that was disappointing," Carly said.

Zane slumped back into the love seat. "I can't believe I used up all my magic on fixing the clock."

Carly patted his knee. "At least my grandmother will be happy."

He chuckled. "Don't think I'm giving up. I'll try every day if I have to. But one day, I'm going to make that spell work."

"You think so?" she asked, sitting next to him. "That'd be impressive, but even more so if you wear the leotard."

"Carly?" Jeremiah's voice filtered through, pulling her out of the memory she'd hadn't thought about in over thirty years.

She turned to him, her heart thumping rapidly against her breastbone. "I think I might know how to find Zane."

His forehead furrowed in confusion. "What do you mean? How?"

She pointed to the grandfather clock, the same one that had been in her grandmother's house all those years ago. "I know the spell he used, and with the coven's help, I think it can take me to him."

"Carly, I don't think—" he started.

But Carly had already walked into the middle of the room and clapped her hands to get everyone's attention.

All activity stopped as everyone turned to look at her. She cleared her throat. "I know how to follow Zane through time. I know the spell, but in order for it to work, I think I need to go immediately. All I need to know is, who's with me?"

There was a low murmur that ran through the room, and then all five of the other coven members raised their hands.

Carly felt a slow smile tug at her lips. "That's it? No questions asked?"

"What's there to ask?" Gigi said. "We're a coven. When one needs help, we all go."

The others nodded in agreement, and before she knew it, her coven, the one group of people who'd become her ride-or-dies, started to pull out their supplies of pillar candles, protective herbs, and wine, because wine always worked as an offering.

Carly walked over to her bookcase where she kept that spell book from so many years ago, and before she could even slip through the pages, it opened right to the correct spell. Already the words on the page were glowing with magic.

And that's when she heard Zane whisper, "You can do it, Car. I'm waiting."

CHAPTER TWENTY

"This looks very simplistic," Gigi said after looking up from the spell book. "Are you sure this is the spell?"

"I'm sure." Carly explained the experience she had with Zane all those years ago. "I don't know why it almost worked that one time and then never again, but obviously Zane figured out how to get it to work again. We have to try. My intuition is telling me that this is the correct path."

Gigi glanced at Sebastian. "Maybe we should wait just a bit until Sebastian can get his PIs on the job. They could find out something useful that will help us. Don't we want to know what we're walking into before we just jump into the fire?"

Carly closed her eyes, trying to settle her nerves. Hadn't they all just volunteered to help her go after Harlow, Zane, and Liam? She was about to argue her case when Jeremiah stepped in.

"I don't think we can wait. They have Harlow and my brother. And what about Liam? He needs to be recovering from his injuries. Would any of you wait if your family was being held against their will?"

"No," Joy said slowly. "I couldn't wait. But Gigi does have a point. We're not even totally sure which side Zane is on. He took Liam, and what about Harlow? Did he take her too? This could be a trap. I'm not saying I won't go. I just want to make sure we are prepared for whatever we find on the other side of that clock."

"Zane isn't playing for the other side," Carly said. "I could feel his emotions. Zane was tormented by what he had to do, not gleefully evil. Besides, even though it's been over thirty years, I know him. Like *really* know him, and I will never believe that he's doing any of this willingly."

Silence filled the room. Finally, Jake, Carly's bodyguard, stepped up. "I'm coming with you."

"Me, too," Mikey said, his arms crossed over his chest. Harlow's guard still couldn't remember what happened on the back deck, and he was furious at himself for not protecting Harlow. The frustration was pouring off him in waves.

"I'm in." Phil stepped up beside Mikey. "We'll do everything in our power to bring them home."

Carly was overwhelmed with gratitude toward the men standing in front of her. This was well beyond their job description, and not something she'd expected them to do. "Thank you," she said simply. "You have no idea how grateful I am."

Jake gave her a ghost of a smile. "Just doing our jobs, ma'am."

"You're doing a lot more than just your job, and I want you to know I won't forget it. Ever," she said.

"Just tell us where you need us," Mikey said, already moving toward the grandfather clock.

Carly glanced around at the coven. The other five women

all glanced at each other, and without a word, they all stepped forward.

"No girl left behind," Iris said, placing her hand on Carly's arm. "Let's go kick some ass."

Relief rushed through Carly as she moved to stand next to the clock.

"Let's set up some basic protections," Joy said. "Can someone move the clock away from the wall?"

The three guards did as Joy asked, and then Grace grabbed salt from her bag and proceeded to make a salt circle. Hope handed out white pillar candles to each coven member and then instructed Jeremiah and the three guards to stand inside the circle, next to the clock.

"Carly," Gigi said, "I think you should take the north side of the circle.

"Okay." Carly got into position and waited for the coven to fill in the circle.

"You take the lead," Gigi said, nodding to Carly.

She nodded, reread the incantation and then raised her hands skyward. The coven witches followed, and immediately flames flickered to life on the white pillar candles. "Goddesses of time and seasons, hear our call."

Magic sprang to life inside the clock, making it glow just like it had all those years ago when Zane first tried the spell. The light fueled Carly's resolve, and she raised her voice when she added, "Take us to the one we seek. Help us follow him through time and space to bring home the ones we love."

A rumble of sound crackled overhead, indicating that their collective power was working as intended. Carly could feel the magic in the air. It was intense and stronger than anything she'd ever experienced before. There was even a pull toward the clock that was enticing, like it was calling to her. She wanted to walk right in and let the magic take her.

"Recite the incantation!" Gigi called. "Recite it now."

Gigi's voice pulled Carly out of her magic-induced trance. She had to focus. The spell called for focusing on where she wanted to go. Since she didn't have the location, she just focused on Zane and poured all the love and pain she'd carried with her over the years into the spell as she recited the same words Zane had used all those years ago. "One of three and three of one, let time carry me until I've found my space. By thy own will, may it be done."

Everyone repeated the incantation.

Then Carly met Jeremiah's gaze, and they chanted it once more together.

Magic rose up all around them, swirling within the circle. It was intense and exhilarating and made her insides tingle with anticipation. Her world reduced to no one except Jeremiah. They continued to stare at one another as the light from the clock grew brighter and brighter, until finally it all but blinded her. That's when it happened.

The air was knocked out of her as she was pulled into the vortex of the magic. Everything went black as her head spun. She was disoriented and terrified, but through it all, she focused on Zane and his last words to her, *I'm waiting*.

All at once, Carly landed with a thud when the earth rushed up and knocked her to a cold hard surface. "Ouch!" she cried as pain radiated through her elbow and her left hip. "Holy hell, that was one bitch of a landing," she said, blinking and expecting to see her entire coven and the three guards surrounding her. But when her vision came into focus, the only person she saw was Jeremiah. He was lying flat on his back, unmoving, his legs bent and one arm crossed over his chest. "Jeremiah?" she asked as she crawled over to him, panic starting to take over. She reached for his hand and was relieved when his fingers curled around hers. She sat up and hovered over him. "You okay?"

He groaned.

"Jeremiah?" she asked again.

"He'll be all right. He just needs a minute."

Carly jerked around and spotted Zane standing in the deserted marble hallway. "Zane!" she cried and jumped to her feet. She ran over to him and threw her arms around him. "It worked. We found you."

It took her a moment to realize that Zane wasn't hugging her back. He just stood there, stiff and unmoving. Carly pulled back to look him in the eye. "Zane?"

He grabbed her arm and tugged. "Come on. You can't be here."

"Zane!" She planted her feet and glanced back at Jeremiah. Two men dressed all in black were hauling him to his feet. "Who are they?" She glanced around, noting that her first impression had been correct and neither the coven nor her bodyguards had made it through the clock. "What's going on?"

"They're taking Jeremiah to his room. You're coming with me," he said and forcefully dragged her in the opposite direction.

She yanked her arm out of his grip. "No. I'm not going anywhere without Jeremiah." She started to run back toward him, but before she could reach him, the two guards and Jeremiah disappeared into thin air. Carly came to an abrupt stop and stared open-mouthed at the empty space. "Zane? What. Is. Going. On?"

"It's Lazer," he said and pressed his hand to her lower back. "Come on. I'll take you to your niece."

"Harlow? She's here?"

He nodded.

With one last look at where Jeremiah had been, she went willingly with Zane, praying that she wasn't making a huge mistake.

Their heels clacked loudly on the marble floors as they made their way down the long hallway, passing half a dozen wooden doors. "Where are we?"

"Headquarters." He nodded to a door on the left. "This is it."

Carly waited as he checked the door and found it locked. Her heart sank. This had been expected. She knew that if they had Harlow, they were keeping her against her will, but seeing that she was locked up filled Carly with rage. She stepped between him and the door. "Tell me exactly what's going on right now."

His sad brown eyes met hers. "I'm sorry, Car. I didn't intend for this to happen."

"For what? For you to be trapped or compelled by someone? We can get you out of here. I swear. I have an entire team of witches behind me. Whatever this is," she waved at the impersonal, far too cold mansion, "it doesn't matter. All you need to do is walk away."

He shook his head. "I wish it was that easy." Before she could say another word, he reached around her and pressed his hand to some sort of electronic monitor, and the door swung open. He grabbed her wrist, twisted her around, and forced her in the room. The door slammed behind them and in the silence, Carly heard the door lock.

"What the hell is going on?" she raged, barely taking in the lavish bedroom with the king-size bed and adjoining sitting room that looked out over the ocean.

He walked over to a second door, opened it, and waved Carly over. "Harlow's in here."

Carly ran over to him and spotted her niece curled up in a chair, staring out the window. "Harlow?"

Her niece didn't move or even seem to hear her.

"Harlow?" she raised her voice and stepped into the room.

The younger woman finally looked up. "Who's Harlow?"

"Just someone who looks like you," Zane told her. He moved to stand behind her and placed a hand on her shoulder. "Carly, I'd like to introduce you to Dani. She's our newest employee."

"Employee?" Carly's voice went up more than a few octaves. "Employee of what?"

"I spell things," Harlow said pleasantly. "And make beauty potions. It's a great job. You'll love it."

Carly stared hard at Zane. "What have you done to her?"

He didn't answer. Instead, he backed up until he was standing next to the door. "Get comfortable, Carly. You're going to be here a while."

She bolted toward him, realizing that he was going to lock her in with her niece without giving her any answers. "Zane, don't you dare leave this room! I demand you tell me exactly what's going on right this minute."

His gaze flickered upward and to the right very quickly, and he gave her the tiniest shake of his head before saying, "We'll discuss the terms of your stay after you've settled down."

Zane's expression was pained as he walked into the next room and then disappeared into the hallway. Once again, the door locked behind him.

CHAPTER TWENTY-ONE

arly stared at the door for a long moment. She hadn't imagined that subtle warning, had she? Certainly Zane had been warning her about a hidden camera, right? Did that mean he was putting on an act until there was an opportunity to break them out? She just couldn't believe that he'd lure her to the mansion of horrors with the intent of forcing her into some sort of magical work camp.

She tried the door, even though she already knew it would be locked. When it didn't budge, she hurried back into the adjoining room.

Harlow sat in front of her chair on the floor, reading some book.

Carly hurried over to her. "Harlow?"

She looked up, her blond curls wilder than normal. It looked as if she'd been running her hand through her hair, something she only did when she was anxious. "Who's Harlow?" she asked in an innocent voice that in no way matched her alarmed facial expression.

"You are," Carly said, completely confused until Harlow tapped the floor next to her, indicating she should sit down.

"Sorry, you must be mistaking me for someone else. My name's Dani."

Carly blinked at her. "Dani?"

"That's right. Dani. I make potions and cast magical spells. You'll see soon enough." She tapped the book she'd been studying. "See? You'll be up to speed in no time."

Carly glanced at the book. In bold letters written in sharpie at the top of the page there was a message. *They're watching and listening. We can't talk here.*

Harlow, Carly mouthed. *You're not spelled?*

She mouthed back, *No.*

Carly forced herself not to look back in the corner where Zane had indicated there was probably a camera. Though she desperately wanted to. She wanted to talk right into it and tell whoever was behind this that she'd never rest until she brought them down. She didn't care what it took, she'd personally make sure they never lived another free day out of custody.

Harlow slipped her hand into Carly's and squeezed.

"I'm getting you out of here," Carly said, not caring about the camera. What else did they expect her to say?

"Why?" Harlow asked, continuing on with her act. "It's beautiful here. Why would I want to leave?" She gestured to the window that had a view very similar to the one from Carly's house.

For the first time, Carly took a moment to wonder exactly where they were. They were definitely perched next to the ocean, but were they still in California? And if so, how far away were they from Premonition Pointe? Carly stood and went to the window. All she saw was the vast sea out in front of her. To the left, there looked to be a cement privacy wall, and all she saw to the right was more of the house where they were being detained.

Carly turned to Harlow. "Have you been outside?"

Harlow shook her head. "It's usually foggy in the morning and in the evening. During the day, I'm busy working."

What had they done to her niece? Installed memories that she couldn't possibly have? That's what it sounded like. Carly played along, trying to get a clear picture of what exactly was going on at the mansion of doom. "Working on what, exactly? You said you cast spells on things and make beauty potions?" Surely whatever it was, it had to be something illegal. Why else would whoever was running this operation abduct people to work and force them to produce his products?

Harlow tapped her bottom lip, appearing to be thinking about her answer. "Today I spelled a handful of daggers."

"Spelled them to do what?" Carly asked.

The door in the other room crashed open, and Liam strode in. He was dressed in ripped jeans and a tight white T-shirt that clung to him. But what really startled her was the fact that all the wounds on his face were healed and he no longer seemed to be wearing a bandage on his shoulder. In fact, he was moving as if he'd never been shot.

"Liam?" Carly met him halfway across the room. "Are you all right?"

"Of course I am," he said impatiently. "Come on. The boss wants to see you."

"Why her?" Harlow asked in a whiney voice Carly had never heard from her before. "I'm the one who spelled all those daggers, and I managed to figure out what was wrong with that acne potion. He said I'd get a reward for my extra work." Harlow waved a hand at Carly. "She just got here and hasn't done anything at all."

"He'll send for you when he's good and ready, Dani," Liam said impatiently. "You're not his only priority."

Carly frowned at Harlow, trying to figure out exactly what was going on with her. Was she trying to leave the room? It seemed to be the only explanation. If that was the case, then Carly certainly could help. She dug her heels in and crossed her arms over her chest. "I'm not leaving this room without my niece. If the boss wants to see me, he's going to have to see her, too."

"Niece?" Liam asked, looking between the two of them in confusion. "You're related?"

Carly sighed. "Your memory has been wiped again, hasn't it?"

"What the hell are you talking about, lady?" He grabbed her by her wrist and yanked her toward the door. "I'm not some mindless sheep. No one has wiped my memory."

Except they had. He didn't recognize her or Harlow. Son of a bitch! Just how powerful was the person who was keeping them all captive? And if she willingly went with him, would she end up spelled too and never remember anyone she loved? A shiver ran through her. She reached for Harlow, but her niece didn't take her hand. Instead, she fisted her hands at her side and watched as Liam dragged Carly out of the room.

Once she was back out in the marble hallway, Carly decided to try a different tactic. She walked willingly beside Liam and asked, "Do you know the name of this place?"

"You mean the mansion?" he asked, eyeing her with suspicion.

"Yeah. It must have a name."

He shrugged. "We call it The End of the World."

"Not Enchantment?" she asked just to see what he'd say.

"Nah. That's the name of the company for the products we produce here."

"What kind of products?" Even though Harlow had already given her an idea, she wanted to find out more.

"Spells, potions, curses. Anything that people want to buy on the black market. You know, things that are less than... legal."

Less than legal? That was one hell of a way to describe producing contraband. "Right. So you sell them on the black market?"

"Of course. Where else are we going to sell a sleeping potion that causes someone to never wake up." As soon as he said the words, he wrapped an arm around his stomach, let out a groan, and hunched over in obvious abdominal pain.

Her first instinct was to help him, but after the casual way he'd just referred to murder by sleeping potion, she really wasn't in the mood.

A door right in front of them opened, and a voice from inside called out, "Liam, show our guest in."

Liam's face was pale when he straightened, and without saying a word, he waved Carly inside the luxurious office space. It had to be at least twice as big as the bedroom she'd been assigned. One wall was filled with floor-to-ceiling windows to take in the spectacular view. The others were lined with built-in bookshelves filled with rows and rows of old books.

"Have a seat, Ms. Preston," a man with a very familiar voice ordered from his place behind the desk. The sun was shining in on him, casting his face in shadows.

Carly squinted, trying to make out his features, but all she saw was a tall man in a dark suit with short gray hair.

"Liam, shut the door please and then come over here," the man said.

Liam did as he was told before moving to stand right next to the man. The man clutched the back of his neck and squeezed until Liam cried out in pain.

"How many times have I told you to never talk about Enchantment's products?" the man said with a growl.

"Sorry, Mr. Price. I thought she was going to be our newest worker."

"She is, but not on the line. Instead, she's going to work in the lab... with Lazer." Mr Price clicked a button and a large monitor on his desk came to life.

Liam let out a gasp. "Why is Lazer chained to the bed?"

Carly stared in horror at her old friend on the screen. He was wearing a hospital gown, and each hand was handcuffed to the bed railing. Beside the bed, a heart monitor beeped steadily, indicating he wasn't in any immediate distress.

"He's going to be our next test subject. It's his punishment for helping you escape last month." Mr. Price gave Liam an evil grin that rivaled any Carly had ever seen in a horror movie.

"What?" Liam's eyes widened, and his mouth dropped open. "I didn't escape, I—"

"Silence!" Mr. Price roared. "No more lies. Your boyfriend in there has been helping far too many people escape. I spent years trusting him with this operation, and that's how he repays me?" The man stepped out from behind his desk and dragged Liam with him. Liam stumbled and barely got himself righted before Price opened the door and threw him out. "Take him to solitary," he ordered the two guards who stood there waiting.

"Mr. Price! No. I won't—" The door slammed, cutting off Liam's protests.

The man turned and faced Carly.

She let out a startled gasp as she got her first good look at his face. She knew him. He was the producer of one of the movies she'd starred in a few years back. "Jim? Jim Valens? What the hell is going on?"

"The money to produce all those movies has to come from somewhere, right?" he asked casually as he walked over and sat on the edge of his desk. He draped one arm over his knee and leaned forward to whisper conspiratorially to Carly. "You're a damned fine actress, Ms. Preston. But you're not good enough to fool me. Neither is your niece." He tapped his keyboard, making the video change to another sterile room. This one showed Harlow pacing back and forth, mumbling to herself about what type of spell she could use to bust out of her cell.

A rage burned so hot inside of Carly, she thought she might combust right there in Jim Valens's pretentious office. "Why have you gone after my niece?" she asked through clenched teeth.

"To get you here willingly." That evil smile of his was back. "Why else?"

She clenched her fists and contemplated attacking him, but she needed answers first. How long had he been running this black market spell factory? When they'd worked together before, she'd had no idea he was some kind of magical Dr. Evil who had no conscience whatsoever. "I don't know, that's why I asked you. What is it you want from me?"

He chuckled. "Oh, Carly, sweetheart, what is it I *don't* want from you?"

Her skin started to crawl, and she had a strong desire to back up, to put space between them, but she held her ground, unwilling to show any weakness. "If you think I'm going to do anything for you, you're sadly mistaken. The only thing I'm going to do is get my niece, Jeremiah, Zane, and Liam and take them far away from here. Then I'm going straight to the Magical Task Force and sending them to your front door."

It was probably stupid to threaten him with the Magical Task Force, or even to confirm that she would not only take Harlow and Jeremiah, but Zane and Liam as well when she left this godforsaken prison Jim had built. But she knew better than anyone that words had power. She fully believed that she'd walk out of there with the people she'd come for.

"Is that what you think?" he asked with a raised eyebrow.

"Yes. It definitely is what I think."

"Hmm, and here I was thinking that I'd give you the opportunity to sign the contract of your life." He reached into the top drawer of his desk and pulled out a manilla folder. "You'll have a stake in each movie we produce with a generous portion of net receipts. The ability to choose who you want to star with, what director you want, and even the writers you choose to have a book developed into a script. Basically at every level of the business, you'll have control. You'll be the most powerful woman in Hollywood. Think of the movies that will be made about you." The sly grin on his face confirmed that he was convinced she'd be seduced by money and power.

He couldn't have been more wrong.

"And what exactly makes you think that I'll get into business with someone like you?" she asked, wishing that she could produce daggers out of thin air. She wasn't a violent person, but if she had the opportunity, she'd stab him right then and there. How dare he try to buy her with some over-the-top Hollywood contract as if she were a heartless bitch who only cared about prestige and money?

"Because if you don't, your friend Lazer... or as you call him, Zane, is going to find himself in a very precarious situation very shortly."

"Why?" Carly asked. "Why is it so important that I sign a contract to work for your production company? And why are you trying to blackmail me to do it?"

"Oh, did I leave out the important part?" he asked, trying for an air of innocence and failing spectacularly.

"Spit it out, Jim. Why am I here, and what do you *really* want from me? I'm sure it isn't to spell daggers and whip up potions." Her entire body was vibrating with frustration now.

"You'll be the face of Enchantment. Bring a real air of respectability to the company. And you'll work on your fair share of potions. Love potions are big, and so are anti-love potions. The ones we call widow-makers. You can imagine the high-dollar amount those go for." He leaned back, a smug smile on his face.

"Why me?" she asked, barely able to keep from launching herself at him. He wasn't only asking for her to go into business with him, he was asking her to become a murderer and a full-fledged business partner in his illegal operation. "Did you target me for this for some reason in particular?"

He got to his feet. "Don't flatter yourself, Preston." All pretense of a polite business meeting had vanished. "You're here because that traitor in there brought you into it." He jabbed a finger at the monitor. "I built an empire with Lazer as my second in command. I was grooming him to take over. He was the son I never had, and then... *then*," he seethed. "I find out he's been the one setting my workers free. He'd probably still be at it, but he got careless with Liam. The fool fell in love with him, and instead of cutting off all contact, he kept tabs on him. And when my man shot Liam, Lazer lost his shit and tried to take me down from the inside with one of my own potions." He shook his head. "He still doesn't know how close I came to killing him that day."

"Why didn't you?" Carly asked, not sure she really wanted the answer, but if she was going to find a way out of this, she needed to understand the way this man's mind worked. "Why'd you keep someone whom you clearly don't trust on board with this type of operation?"

"He's too valuable." Jim swept his gaze over Carly. "You care about him. When we got word that you had Liam, and that you have a special connection to our problem child, that's when the plan came together. You see, Lazer has a savior complex, and it's easily manipulated when the people he loves are threatened."

"So you're going to keep him in line by threatening me?" she asked.

"No. *You're* going to keep him in line, because if anyone ever goes to the authorities, you'll be the face of the company and will go down for any illegal activity. Not me. Lazer will never let that happen."

Carly scoffed. "You really think anyone is going to believe that I built this empire? There's no history of me being involved, ever. That's not how this works."

"You think so?" He produced a large file of paperwork and flipped it open. "Take a look."

She didn't want to humor him, but she had to know what his plans were. Carly scanned the first document. It was articles of incorporation for Enchantment. They had her name listed at the top. There were business letters, leases, equipment invoices, and many other business documents, all with her name listed as the managing partner along with Mr. Price. The name Jim Valens was nowhere to be found. "None of this is signed."

"I'm glad you mentioned that." He handed her a pen. "Once you sign the top document, your signature will automatically transfer to all the rest. Then it will be official."

Carly threw the pen down. "I'll never sign any of this. The answer is no. I will never form a partnership with you. Never."

"Are you sure about that?" he asked with one eyebrow raised.

"I'm sure. You're wasting your time."

He shrugged, picked up the phone on his desk, and pressed one of the buttons. After a moment, he said, "It's time for Lazer's treatment." His eyes stayed trained on the monitor that had switched back to Zane as he replaced the phone on its base. "See that?" He pointed to a man in blue scrubs who had started to hook electrodes up to Zane's body. "I suspect it won't take long to get you to sign the deal."

"What are you going to do?" Carly's heart started to race as she watched Zane twist and turn and buck around in the bed to try to get away from the man.

"Just a little persuasion technique I've perfected over the years." He picked up the pen and handed it to her again. "I think you're going to need this."

Carly clutched the pen in her fist like a weapon and waited for her opportunity.

A loud cracking sound came from the monitor, followed by Zane's body bowing off the bed as electricity was pumped through the electrodes connected to him.

"Stop!" Carly cried, horrified by what she'd just witnessed. "Stop! You're killing him!"

Jim Valens tapped the pile of paperwork. "Just sign here and everything will be over."

Carly glanced at the contract, then at Zane's lifeless body. The crackling sound filled her ears again, followed by Zane's blood-curdling scream. Carly clutched the pen in her fist and took a step forward, but instead of signing the paperwork, she launched herself at Jim Valens and stabbed him right in the neck with his own pen.

CHAPTER TWENTY-TWO

*E*arly and Valens fell onto the desk with Carly's weight holding him down. She had a death grip on the pen that was now lodged into his neck.

He stared up at her, fear in those previously heartless brown eyes. He struggled to catch his breath before he finally reached up and clutched her by the throat. She clawed at his hand and sank the pen in further.

His grip loosened just enough for her to say, "Let go, or I'll kill you. It won't take much to nick your artery, you sick son of a bitch." She was pretty certain that was true. While she was no expert in physiology, she had once played an evil doctor and had a medical consultant on set. She'd learned a lot about the different ways to kill someone during that production.

Valens froze and she could tell that she'd struck the fear of gods into him.

"Let go. Now," she ordered.

He did as he was told and didn't move.

"Now tell that bastard to stop torturing Zane." She jerked her head toward the monitor.

When he didn't respond, she increased the pressure on the pen slightly. His breath quickened, and his face turned white.

"That's right. I'm not playing around," she hissed. "Do it. Tell him to leave Zane alone."

The man trapped beneath her grabbed for the phone, hit a button, and growled, "That's enough."

"Tell him to let him go," Carly whispered.

He glared at Carly but did as she said. "Remove his restraints."

"Yes sir," the man said and went about unhooking Zane from the medical equipment before moving to the restraints.

As soon as Zane was free, Carly said, "Now you're going to tell them to bring Harlow to us."

Those cold, dead eyes bored into Carly.

She dug her fingernails into his skin just because she could. "Is today the day you die, Valens?"

Pure hatred seeped from every pore of his body when he again reached for the phone. But instead of hitting the button, he smashed the receiver against the side of her head, sending her reeling backward.

He reached up and yanked the pen out of his neck.

Carly's stare fixated on the blood pouring out of him and soaking his gray shirt.

When he pushed himself off the desk and staggered toward her, she scrambled to her feet and bolted out the office door. With the sound of his footsteps right behind her, she ran as fast as she could through the mansion, turning left and right, looking for anything that might appear to be the rooms where they kept Zane and Harlow.

Downstairs, right? Wasn't the basement where they always kept people locked up? She hadn't noticed any windows in the rooms they'd been in. That implied they were either rooms in the middle of the house or some sort of basement. She found a narrow set of stairs that led to the lower level and took them two at a time. The moment she reached the landing, she collided head first into someone else.

Carly clutched at the railing and barely kept herself from falling back onto the stairs.

"Holy shit. Watch where you're going," a familiar voice said.

Carly squinted in the dim light at the man and then breathed a sigh of relief when she recognized him. "Liam, thank the gods. I thought you were locked away somewhere."

"Not everyone does everything the boss says. It pays to have friends who owe you favors," he said with a sniff.

Relief rushed through her, and she prayed those same friends would help her with Zane. "That's a relief. Now help me find Zane's—Lazer's room. He's in trouble."

"Where the hell do you think I was going?" He reached out and physically removed Carly from his path and started making his way down the hallway.

"He's being kept down here, then?" Carly called after him.

"Shh," he said as he paused to look back at her. "I'll take you to him, but only if you stop talking. Do you have any idea what they'll do to us if they find us?"

She did in fact have an idea, and it made a shiver crawl up her spine. She put a finger to her lips, indicating that she'd keep quiet.

They crept through the eerily silent house with Liam carefully checking every room before leading Carly through to the next one. She wanted to ask where everyone was. Surely Valens wouldn't just let her roam through his house without a search. Or maybe he had passed out from blood loss and no one was doing his bidding. It was a real possibility. It was a longshot, but she had hope.

"This way," Liam whispered. He led her into a windowless sitting room that looked like something out of a museum with its velvet tufted couches, what she presumed were fake Monet paintings, and shiny gold statues.

"What are we doing in here?" she whispered.

"You'll see." He walked over to one of the statues and grabbed its crotch. Immediately a replica painting of Monet's Water Lilies opened up like a door, revealing a hidden passageway.

"Of course," she said, rolling her eyes at the fact that the hidden passage way was opened by grabbing a statue by the balls. Valens would think that was funny.

"Come on." Liam waved her through into the sterile white hall that looked like every fake lab on every movie set she'd ever worked on.

"He's not very original, is he?" she muttered.

"Price is a dick with an ego the size of Jupiter. He's also a mean bastard who will destroy us if he doesn't find us useful. So hurry up, because there's zero chance that Lazer isn't suffering right now."

"He might not be," Carly said. "I got him to stop the torture."

Liam paused and turned to stare at her, his jaw clenched. "Torture?"

She nodded. "Electricity."

"Fuck." Liam let out a strangled groan and started to run.

Carly took off after him and by the time she caught up to him, he was standing next to a locked door, both hands on the wall as he chanted, "Gods of the sea, of the earth, of the sky, and of the darkness, here my call, fill me with the power to walk through this wall."

Magic sparked around him, making him glow just as he and

Zane had when they'd vanished through the grandfather clock. When his body started to fade, Carly clutched his hand and chanted the same incantation. She felt as if something had tugged at her belly button and in the next moment, she was standing next to Liam in the windowless room, staring at a lifeless Zane.

"Lazer!" Liam called as he ran to him, just as Carly called out, "Zane!"

Liam pressed both palms to Zane's face and leaned in close. "Wake up, baby. You've got to wake up. We have to get you out of here."

Carly reached for Zane's wrist and found a strong pulse. The fear that had been gripping her by the throat fled, and she clutched his hand, holding it close to her chest.

Zane moaned and Liam let out a cry of relief.

"Let's get him sitting upright," Carly urged.

"Can you move?" Liam asked him.

Zane blinked up at both of them and grimaced when he tried to move. "Everything hurts."

Carly glanced around, desperate for some water or some sort of pain potion, but the room didn't contain anything except the torture device Valens's minion had used on him.

"We'll get you fixed up just as soon as we get out of here," Liam said.

Zane got himself into a sitting position and finally met Carly's eyes. His own eyes filled with tears as he squeezed her hand. "I'm so sorry, Car. I never wanted any of this to happen."

"You know her?" Liam asked, looking between the two of them. "How?"

Carly had forgotten that Liam's memory had been wiped. With all the treachery going on in the mansion, she was having trouble keeping up.

Zane placed a hand on Liam's arm. He muttered something about lifting a curse that lit them both up with magic. When the light disappeared, Liam let out a whoosh of air and stared wide-eyed at both of them.

"What... I... Son of a bitch! The bastards tried to wipe out my memory?" he cried. "Jesus, a lot has happened in the past few weeks."

"They did," Zane confirmed. "I tried to stop it, but the best I could do was get Vick to mask it so that I could help you get it back. There was no way they were letting me anywhere near you. They know I'm compromised."

Liam turned to Carly. "Thank you for everything. You were so kind to me, letting me stay at your house and trying to protect me. I'm sorry if I was a dick."

"It's okay," Carly said, meaning it. Now was not the time to hold any grudges. They needed to get out of there. "We can talk about all of this later. Right now, we need to find Jeremiah and Harlow and then get out of this hellscape."

Liam clutched Zane's arms. "You're in no shape to be finding anyone, Lazer. We need to get you out of here before they come back. Before they finish us off."

Zane shook his head. "We can't leave without Jeremiah. I won't."

"You always have to be the hero, don't you?" Liam accused. "For once, can't you just put your life ahead of someone else's? We're in this position because you insisted that I leave and then wiped my memory so I wouldn't come back. You forced me to, even though I was more than willing to stay here with you forever. And now look at us. I'm back anyway and we're both screwed. What are you going to do when Price catches up to us? He'll kill you on the spot."

Carly's heart ached. She knew what Liam was saying was

true. But she also knew Zane. He'd always been the type of person who'd give his life for someone he loved. She'd bet her own life that he wouldn't leave without finding Jeremiah first.

"He might. But if I leave, he for sure will kill my brother. And I can't live with that." Zane looked at Carly. "Harlow is your niece, right?"

"Yes. She's just about the only family I have left that I care about," Carly said.

"She's the reason he came back for me," Liam said with an exaggerated sigh. "Price threatened to kill Harlow if he didn't bring me back. He knows Lazer loves you. Even if we do all get out of here, he won't stop until he destroys all of our lives."

Carly crossed her arms over her chest. "Then we'll have to make sure he doesn't get that opportunity, now won't we?"

"How exactly are we going to do that?" Liam asked.

"The coven will help," she said firmly. "You have no idea what those ladies are capable of. Now let's go."

CHAPTER TWENTY-THREE

"This way," Liam said. He had his arm around Zane and nudged him toward the door.

"I've got this." Zane kissed him on the top of the head and gently pulled away from him. "Thank you, though."

Liam sighed. "You look like you're going to fall over."

"I won't." He stood tall, stretched his arms out and mouthed some sort of incantation. It took a moment of concentration, but then magic appeared at his fingertips and covered his entire body.

Carly was amazed when she suddenly felt the weariness just leave him. And in the next breath, the magic was gone. The circles under his eyes had vanished, and there was color back in his cheeks.

"Holy shit," Liam said. "I'm never going to get used to how powerful you are, am I?"

"Hopefully you won't have to." Zane's tone was full of regret when he added, "I wish I'd never opened that damned spell book all those years ago. This would've never happened."

Carly gasped. "You mean the one you found in that used bookstore?"

He nodded. "I was messing around with it a lot, and somehow that caught Price's attention. That's why he targeted me."

Liam frowned and clutched Zane's hand. "But if you hadn't, we wouldn't have met. I... shit." He ran his free hand through his hair. "I know how that sounds. I just... I can't imagine a life without you in it."

"I know." Zane pulled Liam to him and hugged him fiercely. "I like to think that we'd have found each other anyway."

The love pouring off them was overwhelming and made Carly's eyes tear up. Had she ever loved another person that much? There was no doubt they'd been through terrible times together, and that had to have strengthened their bond. Hell, Zane loved Liam so much, he was willing to give him up so he could have a better life than one where he was forced labor in a sadistic crime ring.

"Let's go," Zane said. "It's time to find Jeremiah and Harlow."

Carly followed behind the two men. Both of them were full of trepidation and doubt. It was obvious neither thought they'd be successful, but there was determination behind both emotions. They wanted out, wanted it more than anything, but had likely resigned themselves a long time ago to the idea that it was never going to happen. Carly vowed to herself right then and there that she would not let any of them down. She'd get them out if it was the last thing she ever did.

The mansion was still completely silent, and it was starting to make Carly uncomfortable. Finally she asked, "Where is everyone? Surely there are more people than just us here? The guards? Valens's, I mean, Price's minions? The dude that tortured you, Zane? Where is everyone?"

"It's a good question," Zane said. "If they don't know anything is wrong, then they are working in their labs. If they do, then the shit is about to hit the fan."

"That's what I'm afraid of," she muttered just as they turned a corner and walked right into an ambush.

An alarm sounded, the obnoxious noise nearly deafening Carly. She pressed her hands to her ears and tried to protect herself, but just as quickly, she spun, her fists raised when she felt more than heard someone behind her.

A tall blonde dressed all in black kicked out, nearly taking Carly's leg. But her self-defense training came roaring back, and she spun out of the way right before she was flattened on her back.

Liam and Zane were both yelling at their own attackers, warning them to back off.

Carly briefly wondered if they knew their attackers, because it seemed useless to try to reason with someone who was already throwing punches. But she didn't have time to give the question more thought. A sucker punch to the gut came out of nowhere, knocking the wind out of her. Carly went down on one knee but then immediately came up on both feet, swinging her fists.

"Back off, bitch," she cried and connected with the woman's jaw. Only the woman didn't even seem to feel it. She charged forward, her fists flying.

Pain radiated through Carly's cheekbone as she collapsed onto the cold floor. There was no time to regroup as the woman jumped on her and immediately tried to restrain both of Carly's hands.

Carly bucked, but there was no getting out of her grasp.

"Use your magic, Carly!" Zane called.

She glanced over to see her old friend holding his attacker down with a magical net. He was fighting back, forcing Zane to stay with him to keep him restrained.

Carly had never used her magic for anything other than simple spells or potions. Her self-defense training had kicked in, but her magic hadn't. With her resolve set, Carly glared at the woman and imagined her tied up with a rope. She concentrated, seeing an image in her mind of the rope circling her attacker's arms and torso. Just like that, a rope formed out of thin air and quickly coiled around the woman.

The blonde froze, eyeing the magical rope with horror. When she opened her mouth and started to chant a spell, Carly visualized duct tape over the woman's mouth and laughed out loud when it appeared and covered her lips so that she could no longer talk.

"Damn, Carly. That was impressive. You could work for the Secret Service with skills like that," Liam said from behind her, admiring her handiwork.

She glanced back to see both of their attackers had actually already been tied up with real rope. "Where'd that come from?"

"They were carrying it with them. Check that backpack she has on," Zane said.

Carly did as he asked, and when she found the rope, Zane quickly tied the woman up. Then he shoved all three of them in the nearest room and slammed the door shut.

They had a confrontation with one more group of Valens's minions, but they ran as soon as Zane started to chant out an incantation, making Liam laugh. "I guess hearing that you can travel through space and time has put the fear of the gods in them."

Carly frowned at him. "Why would they fear that?"

He shrugged. "Only really powerful witches can do that. Looks like the two of you share that ability. Anyway, if he can travel through space, that means he's a hell of a lot stronger than they are. They didn't want to wait around to see what he'd do to them."

"Or they're just regrouping," Zane reasoned.

"You were always the more pessimistic of the two of us," Carly teased just to break the tension.

Liam stared at them and then shook his head in disbelief.

"What?" they both asked at the same time.

"Nothing. It's just that I've never seen Lazer act that way with anyone. It's… weird," Liam said.

"Why is it weird?" Zane asked.

"I don't know. Not weird in a bad way. Just weird for me to witness. You don't get close to anyone."

"I got close to you," he said, taking a step closer to Liam.

Liam gave him a small smile. "I know. That's why it's weird. I'm usually the only one you banter with."

Carly rolled her eyes at them. "Okay, guys, as cute as this is, and believe me, it's super cute, we really need to find Jeremiah and Harlow. Can we get on with that?"

"Right." Zane turned and led them down yet another hallway, and when they got to the very end, he gestured to the three doors. "It has to be one of these."

"It's this one," Carly said immediately, pointing to the one on the right. "I can feel him in there."

Zane didn't question her. He just pressed his hand to the electronic tablet and waited for the door to open. When nothing happened, he tried again. Still nothing.

"They must've changed the code, knowing you'd come for him," Liam said.

Carly's stomach churned with acid. Were they walking into another trap?

"I've got this." Liam pressed his hands to the wall, did the same spell he'd done earlier, and disappeared inside, leaving Carly and Zane on the outside.

"He'll get him out," Zane assured her.

"He'd better, or else I'm kicking that door down."

Zane gave her a sad smile. "You could try, but you probably won't be successful. It's reinforced steel."

"Son of a bitch!" she ran a hand through her hair only to get it snagged on a few tangles. She cursed again and looked Zane in the eye. "I must be a mess."

"You look beautiful. Just as you always did." There was a softness in his tone that she hadn't heard in over thirty years.

"Stop it. You're going to make me cry, and I can't afford to break down right now. Harlow—" Her niece's name got caught in her throat, and she shook her head, indicating she couldn't speak.

Zane didn't say anything. He just took her in his arms and held her against his chest. His chest was much more defined at fifty-something than it had been as a young adult, and all it did was serve to remind her just how much she didn't know about this man and how much she'd missed him over the years due to Jim Valens and his shitty evil empire. "I'm going to bring him down, Zane. I swear it to all the gods in the heavens. He's going to pay for what he did to you."

Silence.

Carly glanced up at him. "Zane? Did you hear me? I'm not going to let him get away with this."

He cleared his throat. "How do you know I wasn't a willing participant all these years?"

She scoffed immediately. "Because I *know* you. The Zane I

grew up with, he would never sell sleeping potions that cause people to never wake up or cast curses on daggers to make them more dangerous. Or any other number of things that Valens was forcing people to do here. If you did, it was because you were forced, or your memory was altered, or they told you it was some sort of other spell. I absolutely will never believe that you willingly did this, that you signed up for this life."

"Jesus," he breathed and pressed a hand over his eyes. "You really believe in me that much?"

"Yes. Tell me I'm wrong," she demanded. "Look me in the eye and tell me you wanted this. That you weren't coerced. That you came to my house to take Liam back just because you wanted him back in your life and not because they used Harlow as blackmail."

"I can't tell you any of those things," he said.

"I know that." She squeezed his hands. "And if there was a reason for me to doubt you, and there isn't, but if there were, Valens already confirmed that you were setting people free the entire time you worked here and he only caught on with Liam. Likely that was because Liam was trying to find you, and they couldn't let that happen. So not only were you not a participant, but you were actively working against them. I'd bet the farm that you worked against their worst spells, too. Am I right?"

He nodded once and then hugged her to him again. "I guess I was right when I told you we'd be best friends forever."

"Damned straight. And now that I have you back, I'm not letting you go again."

"Break it up, you two," Liam said impatiently. "It's time to go."

Carly pulled back and spotted Jeremiah just a few feet away. There were bruises on his face and a cut on his arm, but otherwise, he appeared to be whole. Their eyes met, and it seemed a world of emotion passed between them. Then his gaze landed on Zane.

Neither of them spoke. They just walked into each other's arms and held each other tightly for what seemed like forever. But in reality, it was likely only a few seconds.

"Come on," Liam said gently, tugging at Zane's arm. "There's no time to waste."

Jeremiah nodded his agreement, and they once again took off down the hall.

"Carly?" Zane asked.

"Yeah?"

"You said you felt Jeremiah's emotions. Does that mean you're an empath?" he asked.

"Sort of?" she said. It wasn't a label she'd used in the past, but there was no getting around the fact that her ability to sense others' emotions had greatly intensified.

"Good. Tell us when you sense Harlow."

"Right."

They passed by each door, letting Carly have a moment to search for any emotional signature. As far as she could tell, each and every one of them were empty. They searched the entire bottom floor and when they didn't find her, Zane gritted his teeth and said, "We have to search near Price's office. He has rooms there that he uses when he wants someone close by."

Fear rolled through Carly. "That's bad."

"Maybe. Maybe not," Zane said. "If Price's injury is as bad as you said, he might not be thinking about her at all. The only thing we can do is stick together and quickly determine where she might be."

They were as quiet as possible as they climbed the stairs.

No other search party came for them. And there was no movement in the house. It was as if the place was deserted. Though Carly knew better, and when they rounded the corner to the foyer that led to Valens's office, she wasn't surprised when all hell broke loose.

CHAPTER TWENTY-FOUR

"Go back!" Liam cried, trying to push them back the way they came.

But footsteps were already pounding up the wooden stairs. In moments, they were surrounded by a haphazard group of people, all of them holding daggers that glowed with magic.

"Shit," Zane muttered. But then he snapped his fingers, making the daggers slip from half a dozen of their hands. They sailed toward him, and he caught each of them easily.

"Lazer," Valens growled from his place near the hallway that led directly to his office. "You'll want to put those down, or Ms. Preston's niece will not have a very pleasant stay here."

Carly shot forward but was held back when Jeremiah grabbed her wrist. She ignored him for the moment and seethed at Valens. "If you touch even one hair on Harlow's head, I will hunt you down, and when I get my hands on you, you won't live to tell the tale."

He moved his neck to the side, showing off the bandage

that covered the wound she'd given him. "That's the last time you'll ever touch me, Ms. Preston. Count on it."

"Think again, jackass," Carly snarled with magic tingling at her fingertips. Everything inside of her urged her forward, to take him down at all costs, no matter who tried to step in her way. The rage was so strong that she felt invincible. Nothing like the woman who'd been caught off guard down in the basement by the blonde. No, this Carly was ready to unleash every last bit of her fury until she took down the man who held her niece captive. But just as she took a step forward, the front door burst open and witches, *her* witches, piled in, each of them holding some sort of weapon.

"It's over, Valens," Iris said, striding forward. She had an amulet in her hand and her hair was blowing out behind her like she was a warrior in some Hollywood movie.

Carly couldn't help but smirk. It was the perfect setup for the epic battle scene. Only this was real life, and there was no telling what the outcome would be. The only thing she knew was that she had a badass team behind her and every reason to see this through to the end. "Yeah," she echoed. "It's over. Step aside and let Harlow go before more blood is shed."

"Ms. Hartsen, I don't believe you've been invited to our party," Valens said, ignoring Carly completely.

"I think the invitation came when you had your people attack Carly's guards and abduct her niece," Iris spat. "Also when you tried to involve me in your criminal enterprise. Did you think Grace and I would never figure it out? That you needed us to help you set up a legitimate business so that you could launder all your black-market money?"

"I hired you to help me set up my business, not run it." Valens said as if that made any difference at all. "I don't see why it should matter to you." He was full of curiosity when he asked, "But now that you mention it, exactly how did you make the connection?"

Iris flashed two black business cards that looked like the one that had been left with Harlow's phone. Only one had the word Enchantment and the other Serenity. "You really should hire yourself a better graphic designer. It's incredibly sloppy to have two business cards that are exactly the same with only a different business name on them. Seriously? Once Grace and I noticed, it didn't take too much effort to realize you were using the mansion she helped you buy earlier this year as your hideout. It's too bad, actually, because with a good designer, this really would've made a great B&B for Premonition Pointe."

"You'd be amazed how many people only see what they want to see, Ms. Hartsen," he said with an air of superiority.

His entitlement and arrogance were everything Carly hated about the high-powered businessmen in Hollywood, only he was so much worse than anything she'd ever imagined.

Valens's people all stared at Iris as if she'd grown three heads. There were murmurs of confusion and disbelief. It occurred to Carly that most of them had probably been compelled by Valens to do his bidding and probably didn't even realize the spells they'd been casting were illegal or even dangerous. They likely were clueless like Harlow had pretended to be for the cameras when Carly was with her in that bedroom.

Carly clutched at Iris's arm and whispered, "I don't think his army of staff really know what they are doing. They've been compelled."

"You're a nasty piece of work, aren't you, Valens?" Iris said, pointing her amulet at him. "Call off your people before they get needlessly hurt."

"Billy, it's time to take out the trash," Valens said to the tall, blond man standing next to him.

"Yes, Boss," he said as he cast a glance at the other men around him. He jerked his head and said, "Get rid of them. Leave Lazer for me."

Zane swore as he handed the daggers in his hand to Jeremiah. When Billy flew across the room at him, Zane met him halfway and immediately, the two men were locked in a magical battle.

Liam took off after him, but before he could get there, one of Valens's goons got to him first.

Everyone sprang into action. Jeremiah kept one of the daggers and passed the other five to the coven as Valens's army jumped into the fray. The tall blonde that had attacked Carly earlier was back and targeted her, but Carly grabbed her by the wrist and poured her magic into the woman. It appeared to be like an electric shock that sent the fear of the gods into the woman as it started to completely drain her energy.

When she was lying lifeless on the floor, Carly leaned down and said, "Come after me again, and I'll put you into a coma where you might never wake up. Understand?"

The woman swallowed and gave her the tiniest nod of understanding.

Carly stepped over her and stared into the cold, gleeful eyes of Jim Valens. His gaze met hers, and his eyes started to gleam with anticipation. He wanted her to come for him. He wanted his revenge.

He could try, but he wouldn't succeed. Carly warded off not one, not two, but three of his minions, each time, zapping them with her energy. None of them stuck around long enough for her to drain them to the point of uselessness, but that was perfectly fine with her. Her fight wasn't with them; it was with the man who'd tried to take everything she'd ever held dear from her.

"Come on, then," Valens said, taunting her. "Show me what you've got, Carly."

Magic crackled around her. She wasn't sure if she'd caused it or if it came from the battle raging in the room. It didn't matter. Her only focus was Valens. "I want my niece, Valens. No one is leaving here without her."

"Then I guess no one leaves." The villainous glee on his face was almost too much to bear. It made her sick to her stomach how much he was enjoying this.

That realization propelled her into motion, and she flung herself at him, reaching for his neck. She didn't have a pen this time, but she had her magic and he had an open wound.

But before she reached him, he pulled out an amulet of his own and pointed it right at her. Magic barreled into her chest, temporarily knocking her unconscious. When she blinked her eyes open, he was staring down at her, one eyebrow raised. "Is that the best you can do, Preston?"

She shot her hand up, this time catching her target. Her hand wrapped around his neck, and she squeezed as tightly as she could.

He let out a wail of agony but managed to jerk back. His amulet was out again, and Carly quickly rolled to avoid being stunned with it a second time. She found shelter behind one of his many statues and ducked when his magic took the head clean off the carved statue.

Chaos surrounded them. One thing was clear; Carly needed a weapon. She couldn't fight Valens with her bare hands while he had a powerful amulet. She glanced around, hoping that someone had lost a dagger. But no luck. All she found was a small pentacle inscribed with the shape of a pentagram. She grabbed it and aimed it right at him.

"You really think that's going to do any damage?" he asked.

"It might. You never know what type of magic it stores," she said, but she could already tell by touching it that it wasn't cursed with any terrible spell. It was for protection. The magic was warm and inviting, and not at all anything she expected to find in Valens's mansion of doom.

He chuckled. "You're reaching."

"And you're entirely too cocky," she countered as she rushed him again.

This time he didn't even use his amulet. He just pointed at her and sent an intense bolt of magic. Carly held the pentacle up, and at first, the talisman seemed to be exactly what she needed. But just when she thought she'd tamed his magic, the pentacle exploded and all that pent-up magic it contained hit her right in the chest.

She stared up into Valens' maniacal face right before her world turned black.

CHAPTER TWENTY-FIVE

"If you hurt her, I'll kill you myself," Harlow said, her voice raspy. It was how she sounded when she came home from a concert or was up too late and didn't get enough sleep.

"You'll end up just like her," Valens said, sounding glib and unconcerned.

Carly blinked and stared up into a blinding light. She winced and brought her hands up to cover her face.

"Carly!" Harlow cried. "Are you okay?"

She turned her head toward her niece's voice and squinted. Harlow was restrained in a chair a few feet away. Her curls were sticking up in odd places like she'd been in her own battle, but as far as Carly could tell, her skin was unmarred.

"I'm alive," Carly forced out and winced when she sucked in a breath. It hurt to breathe. She imagined that everything would hurt when she tried to move again.

"Thank the goddess," Harlow whispered.

"You should thank me," Valens growled. "I'm the one who

refrained from killing her. I probably should have, but where's the fun in that?"

"You're a dick," Harlow said.

It was such an understatement that Carly couldn't help the chuckle that escaped her lips. It was a mistake, because her entire body screamed in pain. That magical bomb had really done a number on her.

"I'll be sure to put that in my bio," Valens said flippantly.

Carly forced herself to sit up and noted that while Harlow was restrained, he hadn't bothered with her. "What exactly do you want from us?"

"You already know the answer to that." He tapped the paperwork that was still on his desk. The file that had his blood staining it. "You'll be the face of this company, give it credibility, and you'll keep Lazer in line. This"—he waved a hand toward his closed office door—"fighting, it's unacceptable. You'll sign this and then tell Lazer to round up your coven so we can wipe their memories, and then I'll let your niece live. Here with you if you like."

Carly blinked at him. Was he really sitting there calmly telling her how she was going to ruin her life by giving up everything she'd ever worked for, all the people she loved, and turn into a lowlife criminal? Yes. Yes he was. "You know that isn't going to happen. Instead, you're going to release Harlow and I'm not going to kill you."

He chuckled. "I do like your fire. That will come in handy while you're running Enchanted."

"I'm not running this death-cult company, Valens. Why in the hell did you ever think I would?"

He eyed Harlow. "People do a lot of questionable things to keep their loved ones safe."

"Do you speak from experience? Is that how you ended

up running this... criminal operation?" she asked, trying to get to the bottom of why a powerful producer would jeopardize his life and career for more money he didn't appear to need.

He shifted his gaze away. "Something like that." When he finally looked at her again, he added, "It hardly matters now. I'm in too deep, and I need a face that no one would suspect. Who better than Aunt Serena?" he asked, referring to one of the characters she'd played in a popular Christmas movie where she'd been the favorite aunt and eventual guardian of two little girls.

"You really are a dick," Carly said, making Harlow snicker.

"I'm not here to make friends. Now sign the paperwork," he ordered and gestured to a pen next to the file.

Carly's stomach turned when she realized it was the same bloody pen that she'd used to stab him. She imagined that by using it the blood would somehow make her consent even more binding. There was no way she would or could sign those documents. "Let Harlow go first. Then we'll talk."

"Do you think I'm a complete idiot?" he asked as he moved away from the desk and walked toward her.

"I do!" Harlow cried as she jumped out of her chair and attacked him with a small glowing knife. It slid right into his shoulder, making him jerk and backhand her. The crack was so loud it actually hurt Carly's ears. But she ignored that and ran for the desk, where she picked up the amulet that he'd carelessly left there.

Magic poured from it, hitting him right in the chest when he turned to try to take it away from her. He froze and then fell backward, landing with a loud *thunk*.

Harlow jumped on top of him and pressed the tiny knife to his throat.

"You think you're going to kill me?" he asked, his voice cracking though his tone was incredulous.

"I have grounds. It's self-defense. These rope burns from your restraints are proof enough, I think."

Carly caught a glimpse of her niece's wrists, and although a white-hot streak of rage rippled through her, mostly she was just sad. Sad that her niece had to go through this again. That any of this had happened. That Harlow was now in a place where she wanted to kill a man.

"Harlow," Carly said gently. "I don't think you really want to do this."

Valens sucked in a sharp breath. "You should listen to your aunt."

"Shut up," she hissed at him and dug the knife into his skin, making a tiny cut that caused a bit of blood to pool. Harlow glanced briefly at Carly. "I think I do."

"I know, but this isn't something I want you to have to live with for the rest of your life. We don't need to let the actions of this sick son of a bitch have that kind of effect on you. I can tie him up, and when all of this is over, the Magical Task Force can deal with him, just like they did when the new mayor tried to take over Premonition Pointe and run illegal schemes from the city offices."

"That's different," she said, still staring down at Valens.

"How so?" Carly asked, moving to stand next to her.

"This bastard targeted you," she said through clenched teeth. "And he used me to do it. Don't you understand, Aunt Carly? I'm done with shitty men trying to take something from me. I'm done with all the shitty men who think they are owed something from the women around them. All they do is take from people and ruin everything that's good in their lives." Tears rolled unchecked down Harlow's cheeks. "When are they going to start paying for their crimes? Huh? How can I know that this bastard will be behind bars for the rest of his life? How do we know they won't let him out because he's powerful and can buy his freedom?"

Carly didn't know what to say to that. She was right. About all of it. Jim Valens was wealthy and very connected. Even though they'd provide testimony, too many times powerful men had walked away from their crimes with zero consequences. Carly could hardly assure her niece that it wouldn't happen again. Because it happened far too often.

She sucked in a big breath and said, "I can't answer that, sweetheart. All I know is that we have to live with ourselves afterward. If you slit his throat, will you be able to do that?" It had to be Harlow's choice. As much as Carly didn't want her to be the one to end Valens's life, she also knew that Harlow had to decide to back off for herself. She had to know that she had the strength to walk away even when every cell in her body was begging her to end the life of her abuser.

Harlow opened her mouth and then closed it again. She shook her head and seemed to refocus as she pressed the knife just a little harder. Then she let out a scream and scrambled off Valens.

He bolted upright, caught Harlow by the hair, and sent her straight to her knees.

This time Carly showed no hesitation. She grabbed that damned pen and plunged it right into his carotid artery and yanked it out just as fast.

He froze in shock, and as the blood spilled, all the color and life drained from his face and he fell lifeless to the floor. Carly let go of the pen and let it fall to the floor beside him.

Harlow gaped at him. "Holy shit. You did it," she whispered. When she turned to Carly, her eyes wide and her expression stunned, she asked, "Why? You said we shouldn't have to live with that."

Carly walked over to her, tugged her into a one-armed hug, and said, "He was hurting you, and while I didn't want you to have to carry that with you through life, I have no problem with it. He's hurt you and other people I love. He won't be hurting them again."

The door burst open as Carly and Harlow stood there hanging onto each other. It was Jeremiah. He took one look at Valens before he wrapped his arms around both Carly and Harlow. "It's over," he said. "When Valens died, the compulsion spells were lifted and most of them stopped fighting. The few that remained, Zane and Liam have restrained."

"Thank the gods," Carly said, leaning into him as all the adrenaline drained from her body. "Is anyone hurt?"

"Not seriously," he said into her hair.

She said one more silent prayer of thanks before pulling away. "Let's find someone to make a statement to and then find Zane and Liam and the coven so we can get out of here." She grasped both their hands and added, "I'm ready to take my family home."

CHAPTER TWENTY-SIX

*T*he weeks that followed the battle at Valens's mansion were messy. Carly and Harlow spent two full days in interviews with the Magical Task Force, but that was nothing compared to what Zane and Liam had gone through. They'd been on the verge of being charged with any number of crimes, but when the news hit the stands, that's when the people who Zane had helped escape the compound had come forward with their stories. Apparently when Valens died, all of his compulsion spells and memory curses died with him.

With Carly's help with the media, Zane became something of a hero, and all the charges against him and Liam had been dropped. Some of Valens's minions hadn't been so lucky. The true believers, the ones who hadn't been burdened with memory spells, had gone to jail and were awaiting trial. Who knew the Magical Task Force could trace lingering effects from a memory spell? Carly hadn't. But it had come in really handy when dealing with Billy and the rest of his crew.

As for Valens himself, after going through all of his

documents, the Magical Task Force found a journal that detailed how he became involved in Enchantment all those years ago. It turned out that his father started the company and had forced Jim into it by blackmailing him in much the same way he'd tried to blackmail Carly. His father threatened to kill the woman he loved, and in the end, Valens had reluctantly signed on the dotted line. He'd tried and failed to get them both out of the operation several times, but when his girlfriend killed herself, that's when he gave up and let himself become just like his father. It was a tragic tale that only made Carly sad when she thought about it.

Even after all the details were out for public consumption and the legal battle was over, the media didn't go away. Carly was now dealing with daily inquiries for interviews. Everyone wanted her story. Unfortunately for them, she wasn't talking. As far as she was concerned, there was nothing to say.

They were also hounding Harlow. She had a storied history with the press. After her last abduction, the entire story of her traumatic childhood and the details of her father's death had been in the news for weeks. She'd gone to therapy and had found ways to cope, but it was hard to do that with the spotlight on her. But Carly had convinced her to go back to therapy, and she was doing okay.

"Hey, you," Carly said as she set a tray next to Harlow's bed.

Her niece rolled over and eyed the tray. "You made me breakfast?"

"Liam did," Carly said with a smile, eyeing the waffles and perfectly poached egg. "He's going to make a damned fine chef one day."

"He made my favorite again," Harlow said, sitting up and leaning against the headboard. She picked up the mug of coffee and took a sip before saying, "I think Liam's my favorite."

Carly laughed. "I think he might be everyone's favorite. If he keeps cooking the way he is, I'm going to need to spend double the time in the gym."

Harlow rolled her eyes. "You look the same as always."

"You might need your eyesight checked." Carly winked at her and then took a seat on the bed. "I was wondering if we could talk for a few minutes."

"Isn't that what we're doing?" Harlow asked with a raised eyebrow.

"Sure, but that's just small talk. I wanted to ask you about Sarah."

Harlow's eyes widened before she glanced away. "You know about her?"

"Yeah. Lex told me when we were looking for you after you were taken from the house. She thought Sarah might know where you were."

"Dammit." Harlow put her coffee mug down and then buried her face in her hands.

"Harlow, what's wrong?" Carly asked. "You can't really think that I'd be upset that you're dating a woman, could you? I mean, Zane was... *is* my best friend. I've always had gay friends. I don't understand."

"I... Oh gods. How do I explain this?" Harlow asked, looking a little lost.

Carly reached over and squeezed her hand. "You can tell me anything. I won't judge. I just want you to know that whatever is bothering you, it's okay. I'm here." She gave Harlow a tiny smile. "And if you're dating someone, I'd really like to meet her."

"She wants to meet you, too, and I just..." Harlow shrugged. "I feel like an idiot."

"I promise you, there is no idiocy here," Carly reassured her.

"Okay, this might sound dumb considering everything you just said, but I was afraid to tell you." Harlow grimaced. "I don't think it had to do with you in particular. I mean, I always kinda knew it wouldn't be a problem, but there was this very small voice in the back of my head that kept asking what I was going to do if you were disappointed in me. What if you were one of those people who is fine with everyone else, but not those closest to them? What if it put distance between us and things changed?"

Carly shifted so she was sitting next to Harlow and put her arm around her niece's shoulders. "Babe, that is never going to happen. You're my ride or die. Like it or not, you're stuck with me."

Harlow let out a half sob, half laugh and wiped at the tears that had formed in her eyes. "Thank you for that. But I don't consider myself stuck with you. It's a damned honor to be your niece."

"Right back at you," Carly said, holding her even tighter.

"I think I…" Harlow sucked in a breath before she continued. "I have a lot of abandonment issues and even more with men after everything that I've been through. It's something I'm working on with my therapist, and I guess even the tiniest hint of a possibility of my relationship putting a rift between us kept me from telling you. I'm sorry. I know it must've hurt that I didn't trust you."

"Maybe a little, but I figured you had your reasons." Carly kissed the top of her head. "I understand. I really do. And I also know that telling you five hundred thousand times that I'm never going anywhere probably won't change those insecurities, but be prepared because that's exactly what I'm likely to do. You know, each morning over breakfast, when you leave for a run, or when you're getting ready for a date. Or hell, even in the middle of a boring movie just to have something to talk about."

"Stop," Harlow said, chuckling. "You're crazy."

"Who isn't?" Carly said. "After the year we've had, we're entitled."

"You can say that again." Harlow picked up a piece of bacon and offered it to Carly.

Even though it smelled like heaven, Carly passed. She wasn't kidding about needing double workouts. "I should go downstairs and check on the boys."

"What's going on with them?" Harlow asked, interest sparking in her blue eyes.

Carly knew she really wanted to know what was going on with her and Jeremiah, but even Carly wasn't sure. He'd been staying at her house since Liam and Zane were there. They'd decided to stay after Carly begged them to. She wanted Zane around, and besides, they needed a place where they could get back on their feet out of the prying eyes of the press. Her house, along with the added security, made the most sense. Carly loved having them there, but her budding romance with Jeremiah had cooled as he'd started to get to know his brother again. When he wasn't with Zane, he was spending a lot of time on the phone with his boss.

Maybe whatever had been between them had been because of the tension and anxiety they felt while trying to find Zane. That was a thing, right? People in intense situations developed feelings for each other. and then when it was over, they cooled. It had happened to her on set before. There was nothing like a good old-fashioned set romance for some excitement. But those never lasted, and eventually she'd learned that was never a good way to start a relationship.

But Jeremiah? Her feelings for him definitely weren't situational. She'd always cared about him and still did. All she had to do was look at him, and her insides turned to mush. Holy hell, she needed to get over herself. If he wasn't interested, he wasn't interested.

"Earth to Carly," Harlow said, waving her hand in front of her aunt's face. "Where did you go? You looked like you checked out there for a minute."

"Oh, sorry. What was the question?' Carly asked her, wondering what she'd missed.

"What's going on with Zane and Liam? Are they taking that movie deal?"

"Oh, that." Carly shook her head. Hollywood had come knocking just days after Zane had been cleared of all wrongdoing. Plenty of producers wanted the rights to their story, but they were all lowball offers, so Carly hooked them up with an agent who told them they could do better. "No. Not yet. Their agent is still in negotiations."

Harlow nodded. "I'm not judging in any way, but I'm not sure I'd want to do something like that where your life is up on a screen for consumption by the masses. I can just imagine the stupid shit people will say on the internet."

Carly nodded. "Yeah, I agree, but there's something to be said about having a voice in your own story. The truth is that if they don't sell it and secure the rights to have a say in how it's made, then someone will just make an unauthorized version, and they'll have no recourse even if it's a complete fabrication. I get why they might want to do this. Besides, it will help them with their financial security. It's not easy to start from scratch when you're in your forties and fifties."

"True." Harlow took a bite of her bacon. "I still don't like it, but at least I understand it now."

Carly got to her feet. "I'm going downstairs. Enjoy your breakfast and then invite Sarah over for dinner. I'm sure Liam is making something fabulous."

"Okay," Harlow said shyly. And then just before Carly slipped out the door, she added, "Love you."

"Love you, too."

Carly found Liam and Zane in the kitchen. Liam was behind the counter kneading some dough for the fresh ciabatta he was making. Zane was at the table looking over some contracts.

"New movie deal?" she asked as she sat next to him.

"Nope. Publishing contract." He grinned at her. "They want me and Liam to write a book."

"Seriously?" Carly asked, her heart full for them. "That's incredible. Is it a good deal?"

He handed her the contract, and after a moment, Carly let out a whoop. "Seven figures? No effing way. This is amazing." She pressed her hand to his cheek. "You have both been through hell and back. I can't tell you how happy I am that these opportunities are popping up for you. For *both* of you," she said, glancing at Liam. "It's the very least of what you deserve and if I can help you in any way, let me know. I'll move mountains for you."

Zane chuckled. "You already have. You know that, right? None of this would be happening if you hadn't helped us with those first deals that came in. Without an agent we'd be screwed. We wouldn't have her without you. She even introduced us to a high-powered literary agent, and that's how this ended up on our desk." He held up the contract for the book. "I just want to thank you. For this and for letting us stay here. It's… everything."

Carly reached over and hugged him tightly with both arms. She'd never been much of a hugger except with Harlow, but now it seemed she couldn't stop squeezing people. "I love the fact that you and Liam are here. You know that. After all the years we missed out on, I just think we deserve an extended slumber party, don't you?"

He grinned at her. "Remember when we were kids and I told you once that our meeting was kismet?"

Her heart swelled with the memory. "Absolutely. We were what, ten? And you said that because we both loved the same thing from the ice cream truck."

"Orange Creamsicles!" they both yelled at the same time and then cracked up.

"See," he said. "Kismet."

Liam cleared his throat, and when Carly glanced at him, he averted his eyes. She patted Zane's hand. "I think it was kismet when you met Liam, too."

"You do? Why?" He eyed her suspiciously. "You weren't even there."

"Because he's the catalyst for you getting out of that shitty hell hole. If you hadn't gotten him out of there and sent him to me and Jeremiah, then it's likely none of this would've happened." She waved her hand around, indicating that he and Liam both were living there. "Your meeting was meant to be. Kismet."

Liam eyed her and then shook his head knowingly. He knew what she was up to. She was including him, trying to make sure he didn't feel like a third wheel during their walks down memory lane. "I suppose it was kismet," Liam agreed. "How often do people meet the love of their life after they've been forced into an underground criminal operation?"

The way he said it so flippantly made both her and Zane laugh.

Zane rose and went over to where Liam was still kneading his dough. He slipped his arms around him from behind and said, "You're so damned cute, you know that?"

"And you're interfering with this bread. If you don't step back, I think I'll end up ditching it, and we'll have to eat plain old white bread with dinner."

Zane gave a mock shudder and stepped back. "Not plain old white bread. I think I'll wait to bother you until it's in the oven."

"Good plan." It didn't take long before Liam was setting the timer on the oven. As soon as he was done, he grabbed Zane by the hand and said, "Come on, babe. We have some sun worshiping to do."

"Sun worshiping?" Zane asked, looking confused.

Liam nodded at something... or someone over Carly's shoulder.

Carly looked back and found Jeremiah standing in the doorframe watching her. "Hi."

"Hi," he said and stepped into the room.

Carly noticed Zane and Jeremiah share a look before Zane nodded and followed Liam outside onto the deck. "What was that about?" she asked.

"What was what about?" Jeremiah asked innocently.

"Oh, come on. You and Zane were communicating about something. What was it? Is this where you tell me you're all leaving us? Are my guest rooms going to be empty and no more fresh bread in my oven?" There was a slight hint of panic in her tone, but she didn't care. She'd come to love having them all there. She wasn't ready for them to leave.

Jeremiah reached for her hand and slipped his fingers

through hers. "No one is leaving, Carly. In fact, I think Zane and Liam are here to stay. They both love you and Harlow. If they leave it will be to move in next door after they cash in on all those media opportunities." He grinned at her. "And as for me, well…"

"Are you going back to LA?" she asked, squeezing his fingers and praying her suspicions were wrong. "I know you have a lot of work to do. It can't have been easy being gone for so long."

"No, it wasn't," he agreed. "But I'm not going back. In fact, I negotiated an early retirement with them, and I'm moving to Premonition Pointe permanently."

Carly let out a small gasp. "You are? When?"

"Now?" he shrugged. "I'll need to find a place, but if you don't mind me staying for a little while longer, I'd just as soon stay here until something comes up."

"Mind? Why would I mind?" she asked. But then she stood as a flash of frustration took over. "I mean, it's not like I don't know where we stand or anything. That I'm not always wondering what happened between us and if you're just over it. I'm sure we can just go on ignoring it. But one day one of us will try to date again, and I imagine that might be awkward, but we'll get over it. Or maybe you'll have moved by then. Maybe next door with Liam and Zane and we can watch each other come and go and always wonder what might have been. And—"

"Carly," he said, standing and cutting her off.

"What?" she asked defiantly. "Is this where you give me the brush off and—*oomph.*"

This time when he cut her off, he did it by covering her mouth with his. She was so shocked at first that she didn't even move. But then when his arms came around her, she melted into him and opened for the kiss. It was slow and sweet at first but then quickly became heated until they were both breathless.

Eventually, he pulled back and stared down into her eyes. "Does that answer your questions?"

"Some of them," she conceded. "But I'm not sure what it means."

"It means I want you. I always have, and I'm moving to Premonition Pointe because I'm in love with you," he said.

"You are? Then why have you been... distant these last few weeks?" she asked, searching his gaze.

"I've been working out my own stuff." He sat and tugged her down to sit on his lap. "At first it was just about spending time with Zane and working out my own guilt for not realizing he was still alive. All those years lost... It really messed with me, you know?"

She nodded. She'd had the same guilt and was also working through it.

"And then it was about me coming to terms with how I treated you after the accident." He reached up and brushed the hair out of her eyes. "I was an idiot, Carly. I never should have blamed you. I should've leaned on you. We've lost so much time, so many years. It's painful to even think about it."

She leaned in and kissed him softly on the lips. "Life is painful and mistakes are made. We both know that. We also know there's no way to go back and change anything. The only thing we can do is move forward."

"I agree." He nodded. "The only question is if you want to move forward with *me*."

Carly grinned at him. "Hell yes, I do. Don't you know I've been in love with you since at least high school?"

His cheeks flushed. "I knew you had a crush."

"Well, back then, maybe it was. Now, I'm in love with you. Have been probably since the night you showed up on my doorstep."

He raised a dubious eyebrow. "Really? The night you wanted to slam the door in my face?"

"Yep."

He eyed her skeptically, and they both laughed. "Can I ask you something?"

"Sure."

"Do you have plans this morning?"

She pursed her lips, thinking, and then shook her head. "No, why?"

"This is why." He stood, swept her up in his arms, and carried her upstairs to her bedroom. When he laid her down on her bed, he crawled over her and whispered, "I'm ready to make some new memories."

"What took you so long?" she asked with a wicked smile.

"Only the gods know," he answered, and then he kissed her.

CHAPTER TWENTY-SEVEN

*C*arly parked her car at the cliff that had become so important to her. Her heart was full as she looked out over the sea. The fog clung to the coastline, but the sun was doing its best to break through. She thought it was the perfect metaphor for her official induction day into the coven.

The coven had made her a part of their group months before, but there had never been an official ceremony. Now that everything that had happened with Valens was behind them, she was ready to start anew with the women who'd come to her rescue with no strings, no questions asked, and only pure love in their hearts.

Carly had told Harlow not too long ago that she was her ride or die, and had been for a long time. What she hadn't realized in that moment was that all of the amazing women of the coven were also her ride or dies. They were there for her for no other reason than that they loved her, and she was there for them.

A knock sounded on the window, startling her. She jumped and then laughed when she saw Iris standing there with a wine bottle in one hand and an amulet in the other. Not her amulet, the one that had belonged to her father, but a different one with a bright blue sapphire in the middle.

"Come on, Carly. Today's your day. Let's get moving," Iris called.

Carly grinned, grabbed her bag of tricks, and joined her friend at the beginning of the path that would lead to their coven circle high above the churning sea.

"Are you ready?" Iris asked her.

Carly nodded. "More than ready to finally be an official sister."

Iris clipped her arm through Carly's, and together they walked across the cliff to where the other four members of the coven were already waiting.

"Welcome to the first day of the rest of your life," Hope teased as she gave her a hug.

Carly laughed. "Uh, what exactly am I getting myself into here?"

"It's a cult," Grace said with a wink.

Joy rolled her eyes. "Stop. Carly's had enough of that type of thing, don't you think?"

Carly reached out and took Joy's hand. She was always the one who was looking out for Carly's mental health, and she couldn't even express how much she loved her for it. But Carly always felt safe with the coven and knew Grace was only joking. "It's fine. Laughing about it is progress, right?"

"Right," they all chimed in.

"So," Gigi said as she took a seat on a driftwood log, "let's get to the important stuff. What's going on with Jeremiah?"

Every member of the coven seemed to lean in, waiting for her answer.

"Hmm?" Carly asked. "You mean with his job?"

"No," Grace said. "We don't care about his job. What Gigi is really asking is, did you do it yet? Did you finally seduce him?"

Carly threw her head back and laughed. She'd never had girlfriends like this before. The kind who could ask you anything and you answered because you trusted them completely. Still, she couldn't help torturing them a little. She pressed her hand to her neck and mimicked clutching her pearls. "Grace! Honestly. A girl doesn't kiss and tell."

"But does she get horizontal and tell?" Hope asked, grinning at her. "Come on. We're dying to know if Carly got her groove back."

Carly felt her cheeks heat.

"Oh, she did get horizontal!" Gigi cried. "Look at her pink cheeks."

"Finally," Hope said, leaning back and grabbing the wine from Iris. "How was it?"

Carly's lips curved into a slow smile. "Incredible."

Joy let out a contented sigh. "I'm so happy for you, Carly. You deserve everything good in this world."

Tears of joy stung Carly's eyes, and for once she didn't even bother to blink them back. "He's moving here," she said. "He said he'd get his own place, but I asked him to stay with me and he agreed." She felt herself beaming and didn't even care if she looked like a lovesick fool.

"Oh my goddess," Grace said, all of her teasing gone. There was only sincerity when she said, "I don't think you've ever looked happier."

"That's what getting laid will do for you," Hope added with a chuckle.

They all laughed.

"It doesn't hurt," Carly conceded. But then she got serious and said, "You know it's not just Jeremiah, right? Or Zane and

Liam and Harlow? It's you five and everything you bring to my life. I never knew what I was missing until you came into my life. So thank you. Thank you all for being you and loving me and Harlow with your whole hearts. It means the world."

Her small speech managed to choke up even Hope for a second, and they all took a moment to express just how much she and the coven meant to each of them.

Grace cleared her throat. "Okay, enough of the mushy stuff. Let's get down to business." She stood and held her hand out for a wine glass. "Let's get this witch inducted into this coven so we can get to the important part of the meeting."

"The wine drinking?" Joy asked.

"Exactly." Grace grinned and they all laughed as Hope filled their glasses.

Once the six of them were in a circle, with white pillar candles floating in front of each of them, Grace raised her wine glass and said, "We love you, Carly. Welcome to our coven circle of love and friendship. You're one of us now. Forever and always."

They all repeated, "Forever and always."

Magic curled around the six of them, and Carly finally felt all of her relationship insecurities and hesitations vanish. She'd found her people, and she knew no matter what happened in the future, they'd be there for each other until the very end.

CHAPTER TWENTY-EIGHT

*M*arion Matched walked into the abandoned building on Main Street and knew instantly that it was going to be her new home. Well, maybe not her home, but her new headquarters. There was a feeling the place had that just called to her and settled in her bones.

She could already see the sign out front: *Miss Matched Midlife Dating Agency.*

Marion's days of working with the rich who only wanted younger and younger models of their former wives were over. This time, she was only going to work with mature, successful women who were looking for partners, not young women who wanted sugar daddies.

She sighed, thinking about all the clients she was leaving behind down in LA. They weren't all bad, and she'd done a damned fine job matching quite a few couples. She'd even been to over a dozen weddings for her former clients the year before.

It was just that more and more of her clientele were the

cliché type of couple. Rich man, younger woman, both of them in it for the wrong reasons. Marion didn't want to deal with those matches anymore. She wanted the magic. The ones who found each other later in life and found something they'd never had before... that true partner, the one who complemented them. Those were the ones she lived for.

"I think this property is way overpriced," Grace Valentine said from behind her. "I think you should lowball the seller by at least twenty-five percent."

"I agree," Iris Hartsen said. "It's been on the market forever, and it's going to take a lot of renovation to bring it up to something workable."

Grace was the local real estate agent that her friend Carly Preston had recommended, and Iris was the business consultant who would deal with all the legal paperwork.

Marion turned to them. "How fast can we make this deal happen?"

"I can write the offer today," Grace said as she glanced at her watch. "I've already told the listing agent that we're serious, so he's probably waiting to hear from me."

"Iris? When can I open my doors?"

Iris looked taken aback by the question. "Well, I assumed you'd want to get the building secured before we did much in the way of advertising. Your banking is already set up. We'll need to change the address, but that's no big deal. The biggest issue is going to be the business license. We couldn't apply until we had an address. It could take some time, but I can see about trying to get it pushed through."

"Excellent. Do what you can. I want to open my doors as soon as humanly possible."

"Um, okay," Iris said and scribbled a bunch of notes in her notebook.

After discussing the offer she wanted to make with Grace, Marion left the two women to do their jobs and walked the square of downtown Premonition Pointe. She could sense the magic in the air. It was old and majestic in a way that filled her soul.

The soul that had been battered one too many times and had never fully recovered.

She shook her head. That was why she'd become a matchmaker. Marion had a gift that told her when two people were right for each other. It was like her sixth sense. She just knew. Like she just knew Premonition Pointe was meant to be her new home.

Maybe she'd find peace here in the small town by the sea. Because the goddesses knew she deserved it after the last year she'd had. No more investigations. No more dealing with the Magical Task Force. And for the love of everything she held sacred, no more dating.

"Marion?"

She spun when she heard her name and stared wide-eyed at the gorgeous dark-haired man standing in front of her. She blinked, certain that she'd only been hearing things. Surely that wasn't Jax Williams, her high school sweetheart whom she hadn't seen in at least twenty-five years.

"It *is* you," he said with a huge grin.

Marion immediately looked at his ring finger and nearly flinched when she saw it was bare. "Um, yes, it's me," she finally said and took a step forward with her hand out.

He gave her a strange look, ignored her hand, and swept her up in a bear of a hug. "Damn, it's good to see you."

She hung on and forced out, "It's really good to see you, too."

When he let her go, she smoothed her dress and cleared her throat. "So, what brings you to Premonition Pointe? Holiday?"

He chuckled. "Nope. I live here. Have for about five years now, ever since the divorce. You?"

She glanced over at her soon-to-be office building and swallowed a sigh. "Just moved here this week. I'm opening a business."

His eyebrows lifted. "What kind of business?"

Dammit. Of course he had to ask. "Matchmaking. Are you in the market? You could be my first client."

His gaze swept over her, the same gaze that had made her fall for him the first time. "I'm not sure. Why don't you let me take you out, and I'll let you know what I decide?"

She couldn't help it. She chuckled. "That was a really nice line. I see you haven't lost any of your charm."

He winked. "It's not the only thing I haven't lost." He reached into his back pocket and handed her a business card. "When you're ready for that dinner, give me a call."

Marion stood on the street, transfixed as she watched him walk away. What were the odds? No, seriously, how could he possibly be in Premonition Pointe? The world was really messing with her on this one.

Because Marion Matched had sworn off dating. She crumpled up the card, intending to throw it away. But instead, she shoved it in her pocket, telling herself she'd dispose of it later.

She was still thinking about Jax's sexy-as-hell dimple when she walked into the local coffeeshop and heard a blood-curdling scream.

Marion froze, looking for whoever had been hurt. But when no one else seemed to notice, her stomach dropped.

Not again. Not here. Not in Premonition Pointe.

She closed her eyes, trying to will it away, but when she opened them, the ghost was standing right in front of her and whispered, "Help me."

DEANNA'S BOOK LIST

Witches of Keating Hollow:
Soul of the Witch
Heart of the Witch
Spirit of the Witch
Dreams of the Witch
Courage of the Witch
Love of the Witch
Power of the Witch
Essence of the Witch
Muse of the Witch
Vision of the Witch
Waking of the Witch

Witches of Christmas Grove:
A Witch For Mr. Holiday
A Witch For Mr. Christmas
A Witch For Mr. Winter

Premonition Pointe Novels:

Witching For Grace
Witching For Hope
Witching For Joy
Witching For Clarity
Witching For Moxie
Witching For Kismet

Miss Matched Midlife Dating Agency:
Star-crossed Witch
Honor-bound Witch
Outmatched Witch

Jade Calhoun Novels:
Haunted on Bourbon Street
Witches of Bourbon Street
Demons of Bourbon Street
Angels of Bourbon Street
Shadows of Bourbon Street
Incubus of Bourbon Street
Bewitched on Bourbon Street
Hexed on Bourbon Street
Dragons of Bourbon Street

Pyper Rayne Novels:
Spirits, Stilettos, and a Silver Bustier
Spirits, Rock Stars, and a Midnight Chocolate Bar
Spirits, Beignets, and a Bayou Biker Gang
Spirits, Diamonds, and a Drive-thru Daiquiri Stand
Spirits, Spells, and Wedding Bells

Ida May Chronicles:
Witched To Death

Witch, Please
Stop Your Witchin'

Crescent City Fae Novels:
Influential Magic
Irresistible Magic
Intoxicating Magic

Last Witch Standing:
Bewitched by Moonlight
Soulless at Sunset
Bloodlust By Midnight
Bitten At Daybreak

Witch Island Brides:
The Wolf's New Year Bride
The Vampire's Last Dance
The Warlock's Enchanted Kiss
The Shifter's First Bite

Destiny Novels:
Defining Destiny
Accepting Fate

Wolves of the Rising Sun:
Jace
Aiden
Luc
Craved
Silas
Darien
Wren

Black Bear Outlaws:
Cyrus

Chase

Cole

Bayou Springs Alien Mail Order Brides:
Zeke

Gunn

Echo

ABOUT THE AUTHOR

New York Times and USA Today bestselling author, Deanna Chase, is a native Californian, transplanted to the slower paced lifestyle of southeastern Louisiana. When she isn't writing, she is often goofing off with her husband in New Orleans or playing with her two shih tzu dogs. For more information and updates on newest releases visit her website at deannachase.com.